RUM AND NOTES

A LOVE AFTER MIDNIGHT NOVEL

ELISE FABER

RUM AND NOTES
BY ELISE FABER
Newsletter sign-up

RUM AND NOTES
Copyright © 2020 Elise Faber
Print ISBN-13: 978-1-946140-62-3
Ebook ISBN-13: 978-1-946140-61-6
Cover Art by Jena Brignola

LOVE AFTER MIDNIGHT

Love After Midnight (**all stand alone**)

Rum And Notes

Virgin Daiquiri

On The Rocks

Sex On The Seats

ONE

Brooke

HE THRUST HOME, *her scream of pleasure ringing in his ears, then reached a hand down to—*

"Want another?"

I jumped and slammed the screen of my laptop shut, even as the raspy voice slid over my skin like sandpaper, scouring my nerve endings, making the hairs on my nape stand on end, and my thighs clench together.

Okay, so maybe not sandpaper so much as velvet.

Smooth with a bit of body.

But still sexy as shit trailing over my skin.

"Yo."

I blinked, stopped my mental comparison of velvet to sandpaper and looked up, *way up* into the eyes of Kace. Bartender extraordinaire, possessor of that sexy voice and along with that, owner of a body that should be illegal. Narrow hips, broad shoulders, flat abs, and biceps that stretched the sleeves of the simple T-shirts he always wore. Completing the look was dark brown hair, piercing blue eyes, a straight nose, and lush, kissable lips.

Beyond enjoyable to view. Also, beyond dangerous to my well-being.

Those blue eyes cut to my glass, almost empty, the diet soda well below the line of ice in the cup.

"Yes," I murmured. "Another would be great."

He lifted his chin, snagged my drink, then turned away to refill it.

Kace didn't linger, didn't tend to interrupt—though in this case, I'd probably asked for it, staring at him unabashedly for inspiration. He'd become the hero in the book I was writing, and what a damn inspiration he was. But because of that, I'd been admiring him, daydreaming, plotting in my head as my hero and heroine got extremely familiar between the sheets. It was all strictly for research purposes . . . well, that and also wondering how many orgasms he could give my fictional heroine.

A lot.

The answer to that wondering was *a lot.*

I knew it in the way he moved, fluid and efficient, confidence in every action. Kace might be taciturn with a jawline that was as sharp as a knife, my very own incarnation of Mr. Darcy, albeit with tattoos, killer stubble, and an immense knowledge of top-shelf liquor, but he was also a man who knew his body.

I might be a shy, awkward author, but DNA and three million years of evolution told me he was a man that wouldn't be satisfied without his woman having at least one orgasm.

Hence the reason he'd been the inspiration for my last five heroes.

And the reason I was ahead on my deadlines for the first time in about a hundred years, or perhaps I should say *ever.* In fact, I'd spent the last six months working almost every evening through to early morning in this bar, having stumbled upon it after my neighbor had interrupted my work with his snoring. You'd think that my night owl tendencies would be a good thing when it came to securing quiet—or at the very least a base level of consistent noise that was *not* of the chainsaw-esque variety—but my neighbor's snoring wasn't conducive to that.

Thus, my need to vacate my apartment and its thin walls.

But, funny story, no coffee shop was open past nine o'clock, the neighborhood restaurants closed at ten, and me returning to my apartment had garnered not even a single chapter.

So, I'd Yelped. Then I'd wandered. Eventually, I'd discovered Bobby's.

Not the front room with all the young and rowdy college coeds, but the mostly hidden back room with its warm wood and slightly sticky bar top and comfortable stools with an extra rung that my ridiculously short legs could actually reach.

This was critical.

I thanked Kace when he deposited my glass in front of me, full of ice and soda, then waited until he'd left before I opened my laptop again. But before I could finish the scene—or finish my heroine, rather—my mind and eyes drifted back down the bar to him.

Kace rhymed with mace, not immediately clear when it came to his name badge. It had taken me a full week of visits to discover it was pronounced that way.

Bobby's was a problem.

A gorgeous feast for the eyes, but still a problem.

Luckily, I'd gotten good at ignoring the distraction that was Kace, and my task was made easier that evening because he disappeared through the swinging doors that led into the kitchen.

With a quick slurp of my soda, I got back to work.

The ice in my glass had melted by the time I glanced up again, and my lucky heroine had finished twice.

You go, girl, I thought with a smirk, hitting save and taking a big swig. The soda was warm, flat, and unpleasant, and I wrinkled my nose before setting my glass down. I wish I could say it was an uncommon occurrence, my wasting of a perfectly good Diet Coke, but unfortunately, I ruined them on a regular basis.

"Want a fresh one?"

My eyes flew up from the glass to meet Kace's.

"Um," I murmured. "Sure. But can you add a little rum?"

A flash of white teeth. "All done, then?" He leaned toward me, resting his forearms on the bar, the long sleeves of his shirt riding up to reveal just the edge of a tattoo. I'd seen the whole tat before. On Day 36. He'd worn short sleeves for a change, a bone thrown to the unseasonably hot weather that day, and suddenly my hero had gotten tattoos, beautiful swirling lines crawling along his skin, sweeping around and up his forearms, twisting together and disappearing under the cotton of his short sleeves, tempting a woman to trace them with her tongue.

No.

My heroine's tongue.

Fantasy was fine, so long as I kept it between the pages.

I bit my bottom lip until the mental image faded, kept my tongue firmly in my mouth, and nodded at Kace.

He rapped his knuckles against the counter once, reciprocated my nod, then snagged my glass and turned away, dumping the contents, adding ice, rum, then soda before coming back over to me. He plunked the drink on the bar, but when I went to reach for it, he rested his hand on mine. "What are you working on so diligently?" he asked, and the contact, paired with his eyes locked on mine, stole my breath.

"Wh-what?"

His response was to release my hand, and while I was

mourning the loss of his touch, he grabbed my computer, spun it to face him, and opened it.

"No—"

But it was too late.

It was open, the screen lighting up, illuminating his sharp but beautiful features, and he was reading.

Oh fuck, he was reading!

I made a mad grab for the laptop, but he swept it off the bar, lifting it in the air and continuing to read. My computer obscured most of his face, but not his eyebrows. Those brows kept rising until they were tight sideways C's on his forehead, well above the edge of my screen.

Then he lowered the laptop and stared at me.

"*This* is what you've been writing?"

In fairness, he'd caught me in the middle of a hot scene, made hotter because he'd been my inspiration for it.

A fact he seemed to understand when his eyes met mine. "Jace?"

I coughed. "It's a common name."

"Blue eyes?" He glanced back at the screen. "Tats? Brown hair?"

"Not an uncommon combination." I picked up my glass, drained it, eyes watering against the burn.

"A scar on the right side of his bottom lip?" he asked, putting my laptop down.

Okay, *now* was the time for running.

Something I normally abhorred, but in this case, it was critical. I snatched up my computer, reached into my wallet and pulled out some cash, and tossed it on the bar.

Then I jumped off the stool and ran.

TWO

Brooke

I MADE it as far as the hall.

Because the moment I made it into the drab space, covered in floor-to-ceiling wood paneling, a hand found my arm.

Hot fingers, a scorching palm, and when my gaze drifted down, I saw the swirling lines of the bottom of Kace's tattoo.

Yum.

But that was the briefest thought because ones that immediately followed were: *"Shit!" "Fuck!"* and *"Son of a typewriter!"* In that exact order. Because I'm me, and beyond being cringe-worthy and quiet, although less so in the literary world, I'm also really freaking weird. Scrunchies before they became cool again, obsessed with *Doctor Who*, mom-jeans wearing (though I've never had a serious enough boyfriend to have been at risk of becoming a mother) weird.

So on the scale of odd, I was firmly in the exceeds expectations category.

And normally, I didn't give a crap. I was me, and I liked my nerdy TV shows and clothes that belonged in the 80s. If someone didn't like me, then whatever.

I was old enough that I lived my life by the mantra, *you do you*.

Which meant that I also did me without apology

But Kace was just so freaking cool and sexy and . . . I was just *me*. Me, who was having an existential crisis knowing that I'd fantasized about him, that I was basically writing multiple odes of passion to him, and now he knew the depth of my crazy and would be judging me and—

"Wait," he murmured, thumb brushing along the hem of the sleeve of my T-shirt, making me shiver.

Making me panic further.

I tugged free of his grasp, fully aware that the only reason I was able to do so was because he let me. "I need to go."

"Brooke," he murmured.

I shook my head and slid a step away. "I really need to go." I turned, ready to bolt.

Fingers on my nape stopped me. "Don't be embarrassed, baby."

I stiffened, spun around to glare at him. "I'm not embarrassed."

Lie.

His brow lifted. "Then why are you running off?"

Yeah. Why *was* I doing that?

"I'm tired."

Another lie.

Well, I *was* tired, and I *was* embarrassed, but those two emotions couldn't begin to cover the breadth of all I was feeling. Most dominant among my swirling thoughts was shame. Logically I knew I had nothing to feel shame over—who cared that I'd written a hero—cough, *heroes*—loosely based on Kace? Who cared that I wrote romance novels? But . . . *I* was ashamed, and that made me feel worse than anything else could, which subsequently made me more embarrassed and more exhausted and—

Cue horrible perpetuating cycle in my brain.

It didn't matter if he thought my work was stupid. *I* didn't, and I valued providing some snarky, funny happily-ever-after escapes to my readers.

"Bullshit," he muttered in response to my excuse of tiredness.

I tried again. "It's late."

"More bullshit," he said with a flash of white teeth. "You've hung till closing almost every day over the last six months."

My heart skipped a beat, my thighs clenched, and my panties went damp, all as easily as breathing. Partly because his smile was just that deadly, and partly because he knew exactly how long I'd been coming to the bar.

He. Knew.

Kace reached for me, tucking a strand of hair behind my ear, and I stumbled back a step. *Heat.* His touch had so much fucking heat coursing through me that I wanted to lean closer . .
.

"It's okay," he murmured. "You shouldn't—"

Thankfully that was the moment I forgot about shame and sexy bartenders and piercing blue eyes and found my mad. Mad because I was enthralled with a man I hardly knew, mad because I'd had a man in my life once that had tried to control me. Mad because men didn't get to tell me how to feel.

Not any longer.

"I don't know who the fuck you think you are," I snapped, stabbing a finger into his chest. "But you have no right to tell me what to do!"

That damned brow lifted again. "Baby, I wasn't trying to tell you—"

"And I'm not your *baby*," I said, jabbing him again.

The other brow joined the first, as though this were the first time in the freaking man's life that someone had refused the honor of his endearments. "Baby."

"I said." Another poke. "Not." Another. "Your." One more. "Bab—"

He grabbed my finger.

Which should have sounded gross or at the very least like the beginning of a bad joke, but instead was sexy as hell. Probably because his skin was slightly rough and very warm and made prickles of awareness crawl down the length of my arm.

Then lower.

Much lower.

I tugged, albeit not strongly, because it felt good to have Kace's hand on me, even if it was wrapped around what I'd previously considered a non-erogenous body part. He stepped close, pressing my hand flat against the chest I'd been poking. And I was not unaware of how good the broad expanse of it felt against my palm. Hot and hard and—

Trouble.

"Baby," he said. "I—"

"Ugh! Did you *not* hear a word of what I just said?" I yanked my hand free, anger fueling me as I spun rapidly, only feeling the smallest bit of remorse when my backpack swung up and collided with his arm.

His wince was warranted, considering how heavy it was. My backpack contained the proverbial kitchen sink because I never knew what I would need when I was working. Snacks. (What if wherever I ended up ran out of snacks?) Notebooks. (What if my computer battery died, along with my cell, and I needed to write something down?) Water. (Who knew when the next zombie apocalypse would happen and I'd need potable water?) Rapid charger. Wall plug for both phone and laptop. Gum. Seventeen different pens and pencils because . . . pens and pencils. A paperback and a bookmark, though I could never seem to find the latter when I needed it and usually ended up using some scrap of paper or a receipt.

Anyway, I digress.

The point was, he'd pissed me off and I'd spun away, and he'd taken the hard edge of my laptop against his chest.

But I wasn't going to feel bad. A feat that was made easier when he opened his mouth again.

"Sweetheart."

"Not that either," I gritted out.

"I—"

"*No.*"

I bolted. I'd reached my limit of resistance, of verbal dueling . . . of Kace, and so like the giant coward I was, I took off down the hallway, bursting through into the main room, pushing through the pretty college coeds, and out the front door.

This time Kace let me go.

Which was fine. Totally, *absolutely* fine. He was him (beautiful, dangerous, sexy) and I was me (normal, perfectly fine, just not even close to the realm of beautiful, dangerous, and sexy). So, it was time to put my stupid crush aside and find a new place to work.

Good plan. Smart plan. *Safe* plan.

Unfortunately, I didn't realize I'd left my credit card behind.

THREE

Kace

I WATCHED the flash of red disappear down the hall and shook my head, biting back the urge to chase after her. I didn't chase after women. Not to be a dick about it, but there was no need for me to chase.

They came to me.

And came often.

Snorting at the thought, I ignored my gut telling me to chase Brooke down under the guise of returning her credit card.

She'd opened a tab earlier that evening, and I hadn't wanted to disturb her to return her card while she was busy working.

More bullshit.

Because I'd held on to it as an excuse to talk to her later. I'd been watching sweet little Brooke for months now, appreciating her curves, including lusting after her ass that could only be described as luscious, coveting the rare flash of dimples she tossed my way, and *really* enjoying the blush that appeared on her cheeks every time I came near.

Rare for me.

Because I didn't do sweet, and I definitely didn't crave blushes.

But I'd committed Brooke's to memory six months ago then made sure to cash her out so I'd discovered her name.

I would have asked for her number, too, but I'd had the notion that she would shy away if I'd done so.

So I'd waited. Watched and bided my time and waited.

Holy fuck, *why* had I waited? Of course, I hadn't known what was on the supposedly shy little Brooke's laptop. Wouldn't have guessed if I'd been given a thousand opportunities to do so.

It was dirty.

It was *hot*.

It was—

"Kace! Get your ass back in here!" Brent, my fellow bartender on duty that evening, yelled.

Tucking the credit card into my pocket, I headed back into the bar and focused on getting through the rest of the night. This was my sixth day on in a row, and I was ready to have the next four off. I wanted to sleep, to fuck, and to sleep.

In that order.

Or maybe to fuck, to sleep, then to fuck again, but I'd take what I could get.

It was after last call that evening, after I'd closed down the registers, helped the servers clean up, made sure the inventory for the next week was set when my cell rang.

I wanted it to be Brooke, even though that wasn't possible.

Instead, it was Heather O'Keith.

Brilliant businesswoman, sister of the owner of Bobby's bar, and the pain in the ass reason I'd worked the last six nights in a row.

"Do you know what time it is?" I said, instead of answering like a normal polite person.

Well, it *was* after three in the morning.

"It's lunchtime here," she said breezily as I flicked off the lights and locked the exterior door on the way to my car. "I just wanted to," she continued, talking over me when I started in with a muttered grumble about lunchtime, "say thank you for saving the day, since my asshole of a brother has fallen off the radar again."

Bobby was the namesake of Bobby's Bar and, point blank, he *was* an asshole.

Mainly because he was a flake and kept making his sister, who was supposed to have been merely a silent partner in the bar, step up and all but run the business.

"It's not a problem," I muttered, unlocking the driver's side door and getting in.

"It *is* a problem," she said. "But the problem will be a lot better from now on." A beat. "I bought Bobby out. We'll keep his name on the front of the building, though that will be the extent of it." Her voice dropped to a mutter. "Since that seems to be all he ever wanted anyway."

"We'll?" I asked, assuming she meant herself and Clay Steele, the man who'd swept the notoriously hard-to-tame Heather off her heels the previous year. From what I'd heard through the bar gossip train, and I'd heard a whole hell of a lot because it was scarily efficient, she'd put up quite a fight before she'd succumbed to Clay's patented charm.

"Yes, *we'll*," she said and then declared as breezily as she'd previously mentioned it was lunchtime, "once you agree to become a permanent partner with me."

I froze, finger reaching for the button to start the ignition of my car.

"Um, what?"

"You're the best manager I have," she said. "You've pulled more extra shifts than any other employee there."

"I—"

"And even if you weren't just reliable, you're good at the job, you've been doing more than your fair share, and you're the kind of employee I want to keep around."

"I—"

"So I propose this," she said. "I propose a ten percent stake in the business as a signing bonus and an additional ten percent each of the next four years, maxing out at a fifty percent share of the company—"

"*Heather,*" I interrupted when she would have continued to go on. "Are you freaking insane?"

A pause then, "I'm not going to dignify that with a response. I've emailed you a contract. Take a look and tell me what you think."

"Heather," I began again.

"Bye, Kace. I'll give you seventy-two hours to consider your response." Another beat of silence. "I trust you'll make the right decision."

Then she hung up.

I sat in stunned silence until an ambulance drove by with its siren blaring. That jarred me into action, and I pressed the button to start my car before driving home in a fog. Partly because it was really fucking late and partly because *why in the hell* had Heather O'Keith offered to go into business with me?

Ten percent, right off the bat.

Fifty percent in four years.

Fifty. Percent.

I knew how much Bobby's made in a month because I'd balanced the books more than a handful of times, had done inventory and ordered too many times to count, not to mention payroll and all of the other day-to-day tasks that came with running a restaurant.

All of it, even though I'd only been hired as a bartender.

But I wasn't the type of guy to stand by and watch things go to shit just because it wasn't technically in my job description.

Which might have seriously paid off that evening.

Fifty percent.

Fifty fucking percent was a whole hell of a lot when I'd never had anything at all.

FOUR

Brooke

I'D PUT it off for as long as I could.

But it had been five days and I never carried much cash. Worse, I didn't remember my pin to my ATM card. Ridiculous and totally immature—what kind of grown woman didn't know the pin to her ATM card? I could remember the ages, hair color, eye color, even the middle names and birthdays of all my characters, but recalling those four numbers in the correct order was impossible.

So, it was either go into the bank and withdraw cash in person—which meant, *ugh*, people—or it was time to go back to the bar and retrieve the one credit card I owned.

Also, *ugh*, but I had a plan.

One that involved going into the bar at a time that Kace didn't work.

He was on from evening to close, or so I'd assumed, since he'd been there every time I'd gone in to burn the midnight oil and stayed there no matter how late I'd been pecking away at my laptop.

So my plan was to go into the bar at midday.

Lunchtime barhopping was perhaps not the best expression of my character, but it beat having to look into Kace's eyes and witness the knowledge of me basing the hero in my story after him there.

Including his giant penis.

Which, in fairness, was based more on my hope as a woman of Earth and less on my actual knowledge of said body part.

Though he had worn a really tight pair of jeans that one time . . .

Rolling my eyes, I straightened my shoulders and forced myself to pull open the door to Bobby's and walk into the bar. The front room was empty, so I moved down the hall to the space in the back.

He wouldn't be there. He wouldn't be there. He wouldn't—

Oh my fucking god, he *was* there.

I froze, the long stretch of hall behind me, nowhere to hide.

Kace hadn't seen me yet, his eyes were on a stack of papers he held in front of him, silently reading as he walked toward me. He wore a black leather jacket over a pale blue T-shirt that complemented his eyes. I whipped around silently, started hustling back into the front room of the bar. If I could just make it there, I could run, escape. Hell, I could hide under the table.

I had no shame at this point.

I could not face the man who starred in my book . . . along with my every fantasy over the last months.

Hot and dirty fantasies and the scene he'd eavesdropped on —was it technically eavesdropping if he'd read it? Perhaps eaves*reading* was more apt. Anyway, he'd seen something he shouldn't have, and it had been extra hot and extra dirty and, *fuck me*, I'd been imagining Kace doing all those things to me as I'd written it.

I hustled down the hall, thankful for my sneakers and their stealth. Almost there. Almost there—

"Brooke."

Shit.

So much for stealth. Fuck it; I was going for speed.

I hurried for the front door and—

Warm fingers on my arm. Hot breath in my ear.

"Where you going, honey?"

His touch did something to me, made the nerves fly away, along with my filter. "Not your honey. Not your baby," I gritted out. "Let me go."

"Sweetheart—"

"Oh my fucking God!" I shrieked.

Yes, a shriek. Yes, it was loud. But, for the love of Pete, this man just wouldn't stop. I spun to face him, tugging free of his grasp. "You are freaking unbelievable. You know that? And *that* isn't a compliment," I snapped when he grinned. "That is an expression of extreme dislike and annoyance."

He shrugged. "Dislike and annoyance are only a hairsbreadth away from anger, and I kind of like you angry, sugar pie."

Sugar pie?

Sugar. Pie.

My skin tightened, my spine lifted, my chin rose, and my lips parted—

"Fuck, you're pretty."

The biting retort that had been on the tip of my tongue whooshed away like so much smoke and I stood there, blinking at him like an idiot.

He smirked. "Especially when you blush like that."

My mouth opened and closed, a la a gaping fish. Cute, that. I sucked in a breath, focusing, pulling up my memories of him calling me baby and honey, sweetheart and sugar pie, trying to remember that I didn't like it. Because I definitely found them objectionable and too familiar and I did *not* enjoy the endearments brushing down my skin in his slightly rough voice, just like his calloused fingers trailed along my cheek—

Wait. My cheek?

His fingers were stroking my cheek?

Seriously. What in the hell was wrong with me?

I jumped back, narrowed my eyes, and decided to finally pull my head out of my ass. Breathing through my mouth so I wouldn't be distracted by the spicy deliciousness of his scent, I tucked away the irritation, pushed down the desire, and focused on the task at hand.

People were evil—especially Kace and his panty-melting smirk—which meant I needed my credit card.

Once I retrieved it I was leaving, going back to my apartment to watch *Pride and Prejudice*, and pretend that in an alternate life I was Elizabeth Bennett and I was always authentic, always myself, that I didn't care what anyone else thought about me—especially annoying men—and that, most importantly, I actually stood up for myself.

"I've come for my credit card," I declared.

Yes, declared, and rather imperiously, I thought happily.

Because I definitely needed imperiousness when dealing with Kace.

He burst out laughing.

"You've come . . . for your . . . card?" He bent over, a huge grin on his face, chuckles washing over me as dangerously as his touch.

"Hilarious," I muttered, crossing my arms over my chest and continuing to glare.

It took him several long minutes to gain control, time that I spent searching the bar and trying to find any other employee who might be able to help me. Anyone I could deal with who was not the beautiful, impossible, pain in the ass in front of me.

Anyone.

Alas, the bar remained empty, no one emerging from behind it or drifting down the hall, and because it wasn't yet noon, customers weren't exactly pouring in through the front door.

Finally, Kace's laughter cut off and he straightened, eyes locked on me. "Card's in the safe," he murmured. "Come on." Then he turned and strode back down the hall, leaving me to follow him. I didn't want to, *really* didn't want to, but what choice did I have? I'd come for the card. He was leading me to the card.

I just tried to not watch his ass on the way.

Also note, I failed because it was a really nice ass.

He pushed through a door marked Private, and I trailed him into a small office. It was dark and dingy, a worn desk piled high with papers taking up the majority of the space. A dirty window allowed a minimal amount of light into the room, but it only served to highlight how dusty every surface was.

Kace caught my eye. "It looks worse than it is."

I just raised a brow in response, not buying that for a second.

He smirked, turned and crouched down, fingers working the buttons of the safe, and my way-too-dirty mind liked the way he worked those, wished he were working *my* button like that and—

There was a beep, and the safe door swung open.

He reached in, fumbled for a few seconds, then stood and handed me my card. "There you go, Brooke McAlister."

I took it, shoved it into my purse. "Thanks," I grumbled and started for the door.

"I read your books."

My feet stopped moving. "What?"

"I read your stuff." His lips twitched. "I liked."

Never more than at that moment had I wished I wrote under a pen name. But I didn't. I wrote under my real name because I was too lazy and unorganized to keep track of more than my own name.

I shook my head. "You've read one of my books?"

Kace nodded. "Three actually. You're funny, sweetheart."

"Which three?" I asked.

His brows drew down. "What?"

"Which three books did you read?"

Please, not the Sullivan Series, I thought. *Anything but those.*

"Um." Blue eyes went unfocused as he thought. "They were like fire names. *Heat, Flame,* and—"

"Burn," I murmured, horror washing over me.

"Yeah." He snapped his fingers. "That's the one. I liked them, babe."

"Oh God," I groaned.

He came closer. "You're funny," he said again. "And I'm not much of a reader, but those scenes you wrote? Hot as hell."

I shook my head. Nope. This was not actually happening.

"Also kind of like the male characters."

That was it. I thunked my head against the door. I should have canceled the card, got a new one. Forget that I had the number memorized—it was only sixteen digits. I could do that again, no problem.

"Especially the ones with blue eyes and tattoos."

Another thunk.

"I should have just gone to the bank," I muttered, then stifled a sigh and straightened my shoulders. "Thanks for reading. I'm glad you enjoyed them. I-I'm just going to leave and—"

He brushed past me, leaving me no choice but to follow him back down the hall, but when we got to the front door and I reached for it, he placed his palm on the worn wood to hold it in place. "Baby."

My shoulders went stiff. "Not your—"

"Baby," he finished, blue eyes twinkling. "Got that." A beat. "Come back tonight. Your drinks are on me."

I huffed. "I'm good. Thanks."

His fingers plucked into my purse, tugged out my card, but before I could react to that, my lips barely parting in protest, he'd pushed me out the front door and onto the sidewalk.

The bright sunlight outside was why I didn't react quickly, why I didn't yank the door back open before I heard the *click* of the lock engaging.

Definitely that and *not* the fact that Kace had put his hand on my stomach to push me out. Also, definitely not because the feel of his palm through the thin fabric of my shirt had made me stupid, not to mention wet.

And absolutely not because I wanted to head back to the bar that night, that I wanted him to buy me drinks and touch me again and *not* on my stomach.

Because that would be stupid.

Royally stupid.

Beyond stupid.

And yet, for the first time in my life, I wanted to be stupid.

FIVE

Brooke

"I CAN'T BELIEVE I'm doing this," I muttered, nine hours later, pushing through the crowd in the front of Bobby's and making my way down the wood-paneled hallway.

I made it as far as the doorway before my nerves got the better of me. I could see the crowd inside, an open chair at the end of the bar that was secluded and pushed into a corner, just like I preferred. Less chance for human interaction and closer to a wall plug so my laptop wouldn't be at risk of dying. It also—

"Shit," I muttered, darting to the side so I wouldn't get creamed by a couple who was *really* enjoying their night and thus took no notice of a slightly frumpy, definitely awkward author propping up the frame. I stumbled out of the way, tripping over my own feet, and probably off balance because I hadn't brought my backpack, but I didn't take a header, didn't wipe out on the slightly sticky—*ick*—wooden floor because warm hands caught my shoulders and steadied me.

My breath hitched.

Kace.

Except when I glanced over my shoulder, it wasn't Kace.

No. Where Kace was dark hair and olive skin, gorgeous in a Mediterranean way, *this* man belonged on the cover of a magazine. Deep coffee-colored eyes, lush lips, and giving off serious Idris Elba vibes—and not the *Cats* version, but the gate-keeping *Thor* version with the smoldering looks and panty-melting vibes. Anywho, I digress, but the man in front of me was pure sex *and* his palms were gentle as they brushed up and down my arms.

"You okay, darlin'?" he asked.

And a hint of a southern accent. Hot damn. Move over Kace. *This* was my next hero.

That was for damn sure.

I nodded, not even giving him lip for the use of the endearment. It didn't mean anything, not like Kace's use of sweetheart and baby and all the rest. I don't know how I knew that. But it was some instinct in me, aided by the fact that this man's voice dripped honey. Him slipping in a darlin' here or there was just part of him, part of the southern charm, part of the whole package.

Totally normal.

Unlike me, who was staring at him like an insane person.

"Thank you," I murmured and stepped away.

He leaned back against the doorway and crossed his arms. "Seen you around here a lot, darlin'," he murmured. "Just haven't seen much of that pretty face."

A charmer, but it was reading as so light and superficial that I didn't get nervous for a change. Instead, I smiled and shrugged. "It's got a good vibe for my work."

The sleeves of his T-shirt rode up when he flexed and as pretty as the lines of his tattoo were floating up his ebony skin, his tats couldn't compare to Kace's.

His arm moved again, exposing more of his bicep, and I stopped breathing.

"What kind of work do you—"

He stopped talking, probably because I pushed up the right sleeve of his shirt further when I realized what was there. It had the eagle, the globe, the anchor. It had *Semper Fi*. But that wasn't what had made me reach out, what made my breath catch from more than his ridiculous good looks.

There were tally marks below the image.

Tally marks like my brother had inked on his arm below the same tattoo.

Except *this* one had two additional marks that my brother hadn't worn.

Because my brother had been one of those two lines.

He was a line.

Hayden had been reduced to a line. My throat tightened, my scalp tingled, and I wavered on my feet.

"No denying I like your hands on me, darlin'," the man murmured. "But usually I like my women not passing out while they're doing it."

My eyes flashed up, meeting his, finally understanding why my gut didn't burn at his use of endearments, why I knew they were just cotton candy. Because I *knew* this man. It had been more than a decade since I'd seen him, but I knew him.

"Brent," I murmured, finally noticing the nametag, finally putting all the pieces together.

Six months, and I'd missed it.

Of course, I'd spent most of that time buried in my laptop and focused on Kace. But for six months, I'd missed that my brother's team leader was working in this very bar, and—

Brent froze, hands coming to my arms again and crouching a bit to look into my eyes. "Brooke?" he exclaimed. "Holy fucking shit. Brooke McAlister, is that you?"

I nodded, my heart still absolutely aching at the reminder of my brother, and yet it was almost a pleasant ache because Brent was here, and he was okay. My brother wasn't, but Brent was, and that was a really good thing. "It is."

"Holy shit, darlin'."

I smiled. "You said that already."

"Brookie girl, when did you grow up?"

My smile slipped. "You know as well as I do the answer to that question."

His face sobered, and he cupped my cheek lightly. "Sorry, Brookie."

I placed my palm over his. "It's fine."

"It's not fine," he said. "But I'll leave it for now." The teasing light slipped back into his expression as he pulled back, gaze tracing me from toes to top. "Well, ten years or not, darlin', you're going to let me take you to dinner."

And now his expression wasn't light or teasing, and it definitely wasn't brotherly like the last time I'd seen him before he and my brother had deployed, a deployment that had led to my twin's death.

Not during the mission.

In the aftermath of returning to civilian life.

"What are you doing on this coast?" I asked, shaking my head and shoving the memories down. It had taken a long time to lock those memories away, to live my life without shadows and pain, and to find enjoyment in the simple things.

Losing Hayden had changed everything.

"Looking for a good woman," Brent said with a flash of white teeth. "Just didn't expect I'd find one so easily."

I rolled my eyes. "Laying it on thick, aren't you?"

He grinned again. "I don't think you've seen yourself, darlin'. Do you even look in the mirror because"—his eyes took on that look again, except this time, it was from top to toes—"luscious doesn't begin to describe it."

"Yup," I said, "Definitely laying it on thick."

Brent waggled his brows. "Thick is how many, *many* women have described it."

"Oh my God," I muttered.

"Yes?"

I smacked him, but my lips were curved, and I don't think I'd realized how much I'd missed him because having him there in that moment made something settle inside of me. A sharp stake removed, an ache fading away.

Life moving on.

Brent had moved on and so it was okay that I had, too.

"Brent!"

We both turned and saw Kace behind the bar. Even from thirty feet away with about a bajillion people between us, I could tell his blue eyes were flashing and his expression bordered on deadly.

"Shit," Brent muttered. "I've gotta get back to work."

"I won't keep you," I said softly. "He looks pissed."

"Kace may be an asshole, but he's my asshole," Brent said. "Plus, he always looks like that."

Not from what I'd seen, but I didn't say that.

"Grab your stool, pretty girl," Brent said, brushing past me. "I'll buy you a drink and maybe by the end of the night, you'll let me buy you dinner, darlin'."

"Maybe I'll buy *you* dinner," I said.

He laughed, and I followed him to the bar, taking my stool as he paused at the pass-through that led behind it, and doing this while studiously avoiding Kace's eyes. Brent would get the card for me. I had no doubt about that. I just had to hang out a bit, let him know, and then I could get back to my keyboard.

Good plan, if I did say so myself.

I snagged Brent's hand as he started to move through, opening my mouth to ask about the credit card, but for some reason, the request didn't come out. Instead, I nodded to the tattoo on his arm and murmured, "You added him."

Brown eyes softened. "He was my brother, too."

My heart clenched. "Thank you."

His hand turned over so that my fingers laced with his, and he gave them a light squeeze. "Nothing to thank." A beat. "What are you drinking?"

"I've got it."

Kace.

I jumped when he plunked a glass down in front of me.

"Your end of the bar is swamped," he growled at Brent. "Get over there."

Brent didn't seem to take it personal. In fact, he grinned, clapped his hand on Kace's shoulder, and took off for his side. "On it, boss."

Kace rolled his eyes but didn't comment as Brent picked up a shaker. "Kace!" he called as he filled it. "That pretty darlin' down there is gonna buy me dinner. Make sure she has a full glass all night, 'kay?"

I started laughing. The man was ridiculous and had absolutely no shame. Absolutely none at—

I caught the look on Kace's face.

All right then, maybe not so funny after all.

SIX

Kace

SHE LET HIM CALL HER DARLIN'.

Darlin'.

I couldn't use sweetheart or baby or honey or sugar pie, but she'd let Brent call her darlin'.

What the fuck?

"Fucking hot," Brent said when I moved to retrieve a fresh rack of glasses from the dishwasher. "I didn't expect that she'd turn out like—"

"Get on those drinks." I glared at my friend. "Darlin'," I muttered, shaking my head. "Fucking darlin'."

Brent grinned. "Should try it, bro. Brookie girl likes it. Might get you out of this pussy slump."

I set aside *pussy slump* for the moment and focused on *Brookie.*

Gut seizing, I spun to face Brent. "Tell me you haven't," I gritted out, getting into my friend's face and not giving one fuck.

"Haven't what?"

"You better not have fucking touched her."

Look, Brent was a good guy. We'd been friends for close to five years, ever since we both got out of the military and our paths had crossed at a mutual friend's wedding. But Brent was a player and—

Brooke deserved more than a player.

Also, no coincidence that the more-than-a-player was going to be me.

"I've known Brookie for almost fifteen years, bud. Of course, I've touched her."

I growled.

Brent's eyes went serious. "Shit, man."

I shook my head, shoved a new rack of dirty glasses into the washer with more force than was warranted. I also very determinedly shrugged off Brent's hand and glared up at him. "I'm not backing off."

A raised brow in response. "Not asking you to."

"Good," I gritted. "Because I'm not."

I had just spun back to the bar when Brent clamped a hand down on my shoulder. "Bro."

"What?" I snapped, purposely not focusing on the fact that I was feeling pissed and possessive over a girl I'd known for all of fifteen minutes—because I didn't think the six months of biding my time counted, even if it had clued me into what she preferred to drink and what she was actually working on.

"I served with her brother," Brent said. "Her twin."

Tension gathered between my shoulders, and I knew from the tone, from the look in Brent's eyes when he glanced over at me. *I knew.*

"He—" Brent shook his head roughly. "Fuck, I don't know what to say. It's not fair to tell you he couldn't hang or take returning to civilian life because that's not fair to him and all he went through. And we went through a lot of shit. Brookie, me, the guys, the doctors . . . he was sick, and we couldn't find a way to help him." He swallowed hard. "Fuck me, we couldn't help him."

Now I found myself grabbing Brent's shoulder. "It's not your fault."

Silence. My friend's frame remained tense. But after a long moment, Brent sighed and nodded. "Gotta get those girls their daiquiris." He grabbed a clean blender jar. "Fucking daiquiris are such a pain in the ass to make."

"Brent."

He stopped, eyes on the floor. "I know, Kace." A beat. "Thanks."

I sighed, nodded when he glanced up at me, then got back to work filling orders. But I wasn't really there. My mind was on what Brent had said, what I'd now realized about Brooke.

Had she always been shy and hiding? Or had losing her twin done that to her?

And why did he want to be the one to coax her out of her shell?

SEVEN

Brooke

FOR THE FIRST time in Bobby's Bar, my glass was empty.

I'd like to think that it was because it was Friday night and the restaurant was busy (it was). I'd even prefer to think it was because the bar was five-deep with customers and every single table on the floor was stuffed with patrons (this was also true). I'd also *really* like to pretend it was because of that extreme crowding (I even had people in my personal bubble, unfortunately).

But I knew it wasn't.

I just couldn't figure out if Kace was avoiding me because he was pissed or if it was because he was trying to stop me from getting my card back.

Based on the blue glare he kept tossing my way, I was hazarding that it was the first.

I just didn't understand why.

As in, why he was the least bit interested in a boring, mom-jean-wearing author whose idea of a great Friday night involved Netflix, copious amounts of popcorn and cheap wine, and . . . no one else around. And if it did involve going out in public—because of a noisy chainsaw-imitating neighbor—then it involved my laptop and my fictional worlds.

Except, I hadn't brought my laptop tonight, and so aside from spending some time plotting something that I would probably forget since I was without pens and notebooks and typing something that made sense on my phone was a lost cause I'd learned years ago, I was twiddling my thumbs.

And people watching.

Or rather, Kace watching.

He really was liquid in motion, beautiful and smooth as he moved behind the bar, reaching onto the shelves for a bottle, pouring from it into a shaker in a perfect, steady stream, then capping it and mixing the ingredients together.

I knew from experience that he mixed a good drink, that he didn't just drop a dollop on top of a drink or slosh it into the bottom so your sips wound up inconsistent—either all booze or none at all. They flowed down, and way too easily for a lightweight such as myself, but they were damned good.

And I could use another one right at that moment.

My personal bubble had been more than invaded. It had been thoroughly popped by the girl next to me.

She was beautiful, blonde to my red, long and tall and lithe to my short curves, dressed provocatively in a short, skintight dress that put my T-shirt, jeans, and hoodie to shame.

But we were both doing the same thing.

Staring at Kace. As though our gazes might hook into his skin and draw him near.

Pathetic.

Especially considering I'd been fishing a number of times in my thirty-something years and I never—and I mean *never*—caught anything. In fact, it was so bad that my twin had banned me from even being on the boat with him after the one time I'd managed to hook something. I'd been so engrossed in the book I'd brought with me that I hadn't seen.

Hayden's nine-hundred-dollar pole had been launched into the river and never seen again.

I hadn't missed the raw worms or the casting for hours, but I *had* missed Hayden's soft chuckles as he'd watched me struggle and reel in nothing over and over, the warm sunshine on my face, the damp smell of the river, the sound of the water flowing.

And I'd missed those hours with my twin.

Even more so now.

Swallowing hard, I blinked my eyes rapidly. Usually I was good at compartmentalizing, and I hadn't broken out into tears in public over my twin in years, but seeing Brent made it seem fresh once again.

He wouldn't want me crying over him.

So I didn't, but just as I grabbed my glass, wanting to suck back a few of the remaining droplets in order to distract myself from my tight throat, I suddenly found myself almost launched off my stool. My glass slipped, dumping ice and the remnants of my rum and coke into my lap. Luckily, there wasn't much of it left, but I still managed to gain a lovely wet spot right between my thighs.

Cute, that.

I turned to my right, saw the slender blonde glaring down at me, and parted my lips to say . . . something—demand an apology, blurt a 'What the hell?' tell her to back out of my bubble. But I didn't get the chance.

"Watch it, bitch," she snapped at me, glaring down her nose like I was the one who'd run into her.

Seriously.

What. The. Fuck?

Now, my lips parted further and the words I readied to loose were much, much more R-rated.

Kace got there first.

He leaned over the bar, handed me a towel, then moved through the pass-through and shoved between us. He put his back right in the girl's face, bumping her without apparent concern.

That was because all his concern was pointed in my direction.

"You okay, babe?" he murmured, bending over me to grab the glass from where it had fallen between my legs.

Yes. *Between my legs.*

Kace Last-Name-Unknown was between my legs.

Take *that* Blondie.

"Babe?" he asked again. "You okay?"

I nodded, began dabbing at my thighs with the towel. "I'm good. Thanks."

"Another drink?"

I nodded again. "Please."

One half of his mouth curved up, and he rested his palm on my arm. Sparks. Heat. A shiver that skated down my spine. The man was a fucking drug. "On it, babe," he murmured, fingers tracing over my bare skin and ramping up the sparks and heat. He started to move back behind the bar, but Blondie stopped him by grabbing his shoulder.

"Hey," she said, all sultry and hateable. "I—"

"Why are you still here?" Kace growled.

Her—and petty of me to think this, even though it was probably true—collagen-filled lips parted in outrage. "Excuse me?"

Kace rounded the bar, grabbed me a clean glass, and began mixing my drink. "You heard me." He plunked the cup in front of me. "There you go, babe."

Blondie was glancing between us, mouth still agape, outrage manifesting in a bright—and still petty of me, but I was all in on the petty train, so I was going with it—blush on her cheeks that was very unflattering with her complexion. Finally, Blondie's gaze rested on me, and her nose wrinkled. "You like that?" she said with a sniff.

I gasped.

Seriously? Times two.

I couldn't have written a better bitchy villain than this woman in front of me.

And I couldn't have written a better hero than Kace to step in and save the day. *Not* that I needed him to save the day. But I wouldn't lie and pretend it wasn't nice to have someone at my back.

I hadn't had that since Hayden.

"Right," Kace snapped, and all thoughts of my twin faded. He gestured toward the far corner of the floor, and my gaze followed the movement, watching as a burly man pushed off the wall and headed our way. "So, you can get the fuck out of here on your slutty ass stripper heels and never come back in *or* you can make our bouncer's night."

Blondie seemed to finally realize that Kace was pissed.

Slow but . . . insert terrible blonde joke here.

"I—" she began, throat working hard. "I just—"

"Tommy's bored, aren't you?" Kace asked, gaze directed over Blondie's shoulder. I glanced over and saw Tommy nod. "It's been a really slow night, and Tommy is more of a man of action rather than a man who waits and sees. Am I right?"

"As always, boss," Tommy said in an icy voice that frankly scared the shit out of me.

I'd written big guys plenty of times, but my descriptions didn't do the badassness of Tommy justice. He was huge, he looked tough, and I just knew that he would relish handling whatever brand of B.S. that Blondie would dish out in his own special way.

"You leaving?" Kace asked. "Or getting hauled out?"

Blondie swallowed, eyes flashing between Kace and Tommy for several heartbeats. Then her chin came up and she pushed off the stool. "This place is a dump anyway," she snapped. "Enjoy your"—her nose wrinkled again when her stare traced over me—"eighties reject. I'm gone."

Yup. Bitchy.

I wrinkled my nose back then just before she turned away, I gave her a sweet smile and a finger wave. "Buh-bye now."

A huff, a flick of blonde, *blonde* hair, and she was stomping away on her heels, Tommy trailing her into the hall.

I bit my lip, eyes dropping to the bar top.

How was I the object of a bar confrontation?

Me?

I hadn't written it. I'd *lived* it. Me. Brooke MacAlister. I hadn't gotten lost in my head and I'd actually lived something. Lips twisting up, I met Kace's eyes. His were warm and warmed further at what was no doubt wonder in mine.

But seriously!

I hadn't plotted and thought and written and . . . all the other convenient excuses I gave to avoid life. I'd just been in the moment *and* I'd said something snarky, paired with a finger wave.

Snark and a finger wave.

Holy shit. Who was I?

My smile turned into a full-blown grin.

"Inspiration?" Kace asked.

My grin faded, and I bit my lip. "For once," I murmured softly. "No."

He couldn't have understood what I meant, but something flashed behind his eyes before he turned to look over his shoulder at Brent. "I'll be back," he called.

Brent glanced at me then Kace before nodding. "I got this."

Disappointment slid through me, and I picked up my glass,

sucking back a sip to temper my excitement with alcohol. Kace couldn't understand that I had done something that evening that I hadn't done in years.

Probably because Kace had made me do it before.

In the hall. In the office that morning.

Tonight.

Getting me out of my head.

Kace did that.

He just couldn't understand how important it was to me. From his perspective, I was probably just a normal, perhaps a little on the quiet side, woman who'd gotten comfortable over time.

But I *wasn't* that.

I didn't get comfortable. Not ever. I kept people at a distance, and I was really, really good at it. Aside from my writing, it was one of the few gifts I possessed. Rather pathetic, now that I thought about it as I lifted my glass, started to take another sip only to have it snagged from my grasp. "What—?"

Warm fingers laced with mine, tugged me up from the stool. "I—"

Kace didn't say anything, just tugged me again until my side was plastered against his, and led me from the back room.

Maybe I *shouldn't* have said anything. Maybe this was me getting kicked out.

But then we were in the hall and instead of Kace leading out to the front, he turned in the direction of the office, yanked me inside, and slammed the door.

He was breathing hard and standing really close. Close enough for me to smell him—spice with a hint of sweat that probably should have been gross but was instead incredibly intoxicating. Close enough for me to feel the heat of him sinking in through my T-shirt. Close enough that our lips were only a hairsbreadth apart.

"Kace," I murmured.

"What, babe?"

"This is crazy."

He leaned closer so that his next words brushed against my mouth. "What's crazy?"

The power of Kace being what it was—his ability to draw me out of my head, to have me living and reacting in real-time even though I didn't even know him—had me blurting out something I never would have said before.

"How much I want you."

He inhaled sharply.

"Kiss me, Kace."

EIGHT

Brooke

KACE INHALED AGAIN, a sharp little suck of air that seemed to draw my lips closer. "Babe," he murmured, leaning into me. "I—"

My hands wove around his neck, one of my legs around his waist. My spine was flush against the hard surface of the door, but I didn't notice, not when all of the *good* hard of Kace was pressed to my front.

"Your mouth," I said, heart pounding. "Please, let me have it."

"Fuck," he growled.

And then he let me have it.

His lips slammed against mine, tongue shoving into my mouth, teeth nipping, hands sliding up to cup my jaw and angle it. Flames were swirling in my stomach, expanding in all directions, engulfing me in the haze of a seriously perfect kiss. At least until there was a knock on the door, just above my head.

I didn't hear it at first, didn't feel the vibration of it through the office door.

Not until the knock turned into pounding.

Then I realized what I'd been hearing. Then I realized what I was *doing*.

With Kace.

His eyes had darkened to navy, his lips were swollen and red, no doubt the same as mine. Or maybe mine were worse considering I was a redhead and my skin bruised easily on the best of days. Kace's kiss could also be considered the best—as in the best of my life—but it hadn't exactly been gentle.

"Babe," he murmured, brushing a thumb over the corner of my mouth. "I—"

The knocking came again, but this time it was paired with a voice.

With *Brent's* voice.

"Kace, man," he called through the door. "I'm sorry to . . . well, we got a situation out here."

"Handle it," Kace snapped.

"I think it's best that you're the one—"

"Fuck," he muttered. Then louder, though slightly calmer. "One minute, Brent. Hold down the fort for one more minute."

"On it."

I listened to Brent's footsteps disappear into the background noise of the bar. Kace touched my cheek, stared deeply into my eyes for a long moment, searching for . . . something I didn't think I could comprehend. But whatever he was looking for, he appeared to find it because he dropped his hand, turned for the safe, and fiddled with the buttons again, and opened it.

Then he put my credit card in my hand.

"My number's on the back," he murmured.

He nudged me out of the way, opened the door, and was gone before I'd managed to turn over the card and see the Post-It with his number secured onto the back of that rectangular piece of plastic.

Kace had given me his number.

He'd kissed me.

He'd touched me with gentleness and heat.

My lips curved. My heart skipped a beat.

This living in the real world stuff could be awesome sometimes.

NINE

Kace

I STRODE out into the hallway, cock threatening to break in half, brain hazy, fingers aching to grab Brooke's hand and lead her over to the desk, all from one simple kiss.

A hell of a kiss.

But also just that.

No heavy petting, no getting to second base, or even first for that matter.

Just her mouth on mine, her tongue against mine.

And it was the best *fucking* ever.

Which is probably why I didn't see who was standing with Brent at the door that led into the back room until I was mere feet away.

Tabitha.

Fucking hell.

Brent was right. I was the only one who had ever been able to contain Tabitha, and that was on the rare occasion that she allowed me to do so. She was a bitch, plain and simple. High maintenance, rude to every other being on the planet, and beautiful, if a man liked an ice princess.

I *had* liked an ice princess. Once. When the memories had gotten to be too much, when I'd had two too many shots of whiskey and decided to risk frostbite on my dick. The sex had been exactly what I'd thought it would be when I was sober.

Selfish on her part. And cold. Almost mechanical.

I'd been her sex toy.

Which wasn't necessarily a bad thing. I could do sex toy, loved being that to a woman. But when I was *just* that, just a hard cock engaged to get her off, then I didn't like it.

I wanted to mean something to someone.

Look at me with all the feelings.

I closed the distance between us and nodded at Brent. "Man the bar."

He nodded and clapped a hand on my shoulder, muttering, "Good luck."

I waited a beat for him to leave then turned to Tabitha. "If you're here for a drink, get one, sit your ass on a stool, and then get the fuck out. If you're here to stir shit up, then skip all that and just get the fuck out."

Her outraged breath was loud, her green eyes narrowed. "You—" But her words cut off, calculation coming into her expression. I watched her brightly painted lips press flat before she flicked her ponytail forward over her breasts, a move designed to draw attention to the serious cleavage she was flashing.

A nice view.

But because they belonged to Tabitha, they did absolutely nothing for me.

That move had ended when she'd shown up to the bar "pregnant" just a few days after we'd boned and way too early for me to be the father.

Beautiful, she might be. Calculating, definitely. Mathematically and biologically inclined, not so much.

"Well?" I asked when she didn't say anything further. "If you're *pregnant* again, I'd suggest you double-check your addition and avoid alcohol in the meantime."

"You've always been such an asshole," she snapped. "I don't know what I thought I saw in you—"

"I do," I muttered.

A man to be led around by his dick and cater to her every whim.

"Excuse me."

Brooke's soft voice slid down my spine, warming my back, and it was such a different sensation from what was in front of me that it was almost comical.

"Staying for one more, babe?" I asked softly, brushing my knuckles along her jaw.

Her cheeks went pink, and she nibbled on the corner of her mouth. I'd seen her do that a few times when she was working, had barely resisted the urge to lean over the bar top and take a nibble myself. Seeing her doing it right in front of me? Fucking irresistible.

I bent, pressed my lips to hers for a short, hard kiss that was the second best of my life.

And only second best because it didn't have tongue. Oh, and also because Tabitha was there, frosting us out.

"Seriously?" she snapped as I pulled back. "You're with *that?*"

Brooke stiffened and made as though she were going to rush by us, running again, though this time, I totally understood the need. But *this* time, it wasn't going to happen. I wouldn't let Tabitha make Brooke feel like shit, just because she was a fucking bitch.

"She's fat and ug—"

"Out."

Tabitha blinked. "Excuse me?"

Two women. Same words. So totally fucking different.

That was the moment I decided I was going to keep sweet little Brooke.

I snaked an arm around Brooke's waist, tugged her to my side, and did something I really hated. I repeated myself. "Out," I said again, though this time I gestured for Tommy, who'd poked his head into the hall. "You can escort this one out."

"I'm not leaving!" Tabitha snapped.

"Or you can call Ben from the PD to come pick her up."

"This is a public—"

"Actually, no," I said. "This is a private business, and we have the right to refuse service to anyone, but most especially to assholes."

Tabitha's lips parted, but before she got out any further venom, I stage-whispered, "It's you, Tabitha. *You're* the asshole."

"I've never—"

"Save it," I said and nodded to Tommy, who took her arm. "And do yourself a favor. Don't come back."

"I'm not leaving!"

I pulled out my phone, hit the number I had on speed dial because Ben worked graveyards. "Hey, it's me. I've got trouble at Bobby's."

"Give me five, and I'm there," Ben said.

"Thanks." I hung up, glanced at Tommy. "Five minutes."

He nodded.

"What's five minutes?"

I didn't bother to answer Tabitha, just nudged Brooke in the direction of the back room and to her stool. Then I poured her a fresh rum and Coke, deliberately keeping my gaze off what was happening in the hall.

I could still hear though.

In escalating volume.

Brooke's fingers trembled when she picked up her glass. "Does she come here often?" she asked quietly.

Laughter bubbled up in my throat, and I couldn't stop myself from pressing a smiling kiss to her mouth. "Babe," I said, loving that she hadn't given me shit about the endearment all night, that she was letting me in enough to call her that. "You're fucking hilarious."

Pink on her cheeks, blue eyes dropping to the bar.

Quiet again. Shy again.

Damn, I liked her.

But what I would like a lot more would be if she could accept a compliment without getting all embarrassed on me.

Still, I'd nudged up a corner of that shy, had slid in the barest inch. I could get her there.

Could get deeper.

She glanced up at me, nibbled on her mouth again. "I like your laugh."

Yes, I was going to get deep.

Deep enough that I wasn't going to let her go.

Her effect was remarkable enough, unnerving enough that none of those thoughts had struck me as the least bit dirty until she stroked one finger down the back of my hand and smiled up at me shyly. "Thanks for sticking up for me."

"She's a bitch."

Brooke shrugged. "It's a common affliction."

"Also, you're beautiful, babe."

Her blush darkened and she shifted on her stool, crossing and re-crossing her legs.

Yeah, I was going to get deep in there, too.

Deep in her mind, her heart, and deep between her thighs.

But first I had to get my customers settled, tell Brent to back off, and then I was going to keep pushing my way past those walls until I got to the sweet, soft center of Brooke.

Then I was never leaving.

TEN

Brooke

WHAT THE FUCK was I doing?

I like your laugh?

God, I was the biggest nerd in the history of all nerds.

But then there was the other, the one I wasn't allowing myself to think about.

Also, you're beautiful, babe.

Simple as that. An easy compliment, freely given. Except that his eyes had heated when he'd said it, telling me that while it had been freely given, he wanted more. More with me.

How was this my life?

Sexy, gorgeous, protective men weren't interested in me. I just—

A shadow crossed in front of me, and I realized I'd been staring at the bar top for quite some time trying to sort out my head. I glanced up, saw that Brent had come over. He rounded the counter, plopped himself on the stool next to me.

"Still on for dinner, darlin'?" he asked. "I get off in an hour."

I glanced at my phone. "That'll be two in the morning."

He shrugged. "Something is always open."

I smirked. "In San Francisco, maybe. But in this town? Bobby's is out."

Brent laughed. "Maybe. But we do have a twenty-four-hour McDonald's."

"Barf." I chuckled, and Kace came over, glaring daggers. "Though, you would be a cheap date, and I love their fries."

"And apple pies, darlin'," he murmured, eyes glinting with amusement. "If I'm remembering correctly, you used to down those."

"Not as good as your mama's," I said with a laugh. "But I wouldn't turn one down."

He nudged my shoulder with his. "So, it's a date."

"Brent," Kace snapped.

Brent didn't jump, not like I did, almost falling off my stool. He caught my shoulders before I could and raised a brow in question. He didn't turn toward Kace, staying focused on me, and I knew he wouldn't move until I let him know it was okay.

"We'll catch up another time," I murmured. "As old friends do, and when it's not two in the morning."

His other brow lifted at the *friends* comment, but he nodded and his expression softened. "Gonna hold you to that, darlin'."

He stood and moved toward Kace. "Seems my friend and I will catch up another time." A light punch to Kace's shoulder. "I guess I'll have to be the one who backs off, huh?"

Kace grunted.

Brent shook his head. "Fucking pretty boys. Win every time."

Kace didn't even acknowledge him.

"Brent," I said, reaching my hand out as if I could reach across the bar and stop him. He was my brother's friend, had been mine, and even if I'd only seen him for the first time in a decade that evening, I still didn't want to hurt his feelings.

But Brent just smiled at me. "Pretty clear there's something between you two, darlin'. I figure I should let you sort that out." His smile widened. "Then I'll swoop in and—"

"Close up," Kace snapped, shoving him hard in the opposite direction.

"This new management job has gone to your head."

Kace rolled his eyes but didn't say anything further. Probably because Brent headed to the other end of the bar and appeared to begin doing whatever closing up entailed.

"You know," I muttered as Kace began stacking glasses. "I may write alpha heroes, but I can't exactly say I like having a man act like one in my life."

He arranged the glasses in a blue plastic tray, not looking up at me. "I'm not acting," he said and lifted the tray effortlessly, the pale gray of his thermal bunching around his arms and *ho mama*—part of me thought that if those arms were a side effect of alpha, I'd take it all day long.

Or night.

Or—

"You're staring, babe."

I blinked. "Also, I'm not your—"

"Nope."

My brows drew together. "What?"

"I've used babe with you thirteen times"—he spun, stuck the rack in the drawer that washed the glasses—"now fourteen. You didn't voice a protest until now, so babe stays."

"What?" I asked, aghast. "Th-that's absolutely ridiculous."

"No," he said, coming around the bar and crowding into me. "It's Brooke. It's babe. It's sweetheart, if I catch you in a weak moment."

My jaw dropped open. "I—"

"Babe."

"We don't know each other."

"You've been sitting in my bar for six months now."

"And probably exchanged less than a hundred words in that time."

"Words are a waste of time."

I gasped. That was blasphemy.

He cupped my cheek. "Not your words, babe. But the bull-shit people spin for each other. *Your* words have value."

My heart was pounding in my chest, those being some of the most romantic words I'd ever heard. "This doesn't make any sense. You." I shook my head, trying desperately to clear it. "Me."

Blue eyes turned to ice. "Is this because of Tabitha?"

I frowned. "The girl from the hall?" A shake of my head. "No." Well, yes, I supposed in a way, it was. She fit with Kace while I—

"I've kissed a lot of women in my life, but none of their mouths felt like yours."

Was this man for real?

His hands cupped my elbows. "You ever had a kiss like that, babe?"

Wordlessly, I shook my head again.

"Then it's settled."

What? *Nothing* was settled. Nothing made sense. This was absolute insanity and—

"You're with me."

I had the distinct feeling that my jaw had dropped open and remained open. I *never* wrote stupid heroines who just went along with a man without questions and answers, without collaboration and a fair share of attitude, but I had the feeling in that moment I was acting like a complete ninny.

I couldn't even force out anything else before Kace's thumb was on my chin, gently closing it.

"Till we figure out what this thing between us is, you're mine, babe."

And total ninny that I was, I didn't have a pithy or snarky response to that. Instead, I leaned into the contact, smiled, and nodded.

"Okay," I whispered.

———

I WAS AT MY KEYBOARD, typing away like I'd had ten espressos in the span of an hour, the words flying from my fingers and onto the screen almost more rapidly than my brain could process.

I had all the feelings.

ALL.

It was five in the morning, and Kace had kept me at the bar until he'd finished closing up. Brent left just after two, but not before giving me a quick hug, a knowing look, and a "Call me if you need me, darlin'."

I hadn't stayed because Kace had handcuffed me to the stool and kept me hostage—though I might as well have been. Instead, I'd stayed because he'd unleashed his smile, his teasing. Because he'd given me a glimpse of charm.

I'd liked him before—gentle, beautiful, but almost untouchable.

Now? *All* of that, except with a wicked sense of humor that had me bursting into laughter more than a few times, and that untouchable air was gone. Poof. Like so much smoke. He hadn't kissed me again, but he'd *touched.*

A brush down my arm when he moved passed me to check the tables.

A tug on my ponytail when he came back.

A squeeze on my shoulder.

Fingers on the back of my neck.

On my jaw.

Down my nose.

I'd cataloged them all, tucked them safely into my brain to dish over later, because I was in deep.

I *liked* him.

Hence the feelings. Hence the typing. Hence the tactile and mental vomiting of thoughts onto my laptop.

My heroine suddenly became me—okay, lie, Lexy had already been me for a while. But she worked out her/*my* confusion as the pages added up. And though it took me a couple of chapters to work through it (with the hero/*Kace* telling her she was beautiful and had value—no clue where that came from. *Snort.*) I decided I needed to be done with the comparisons and putting myself down.

I had value.

The things I did had value.

I'd somehow forgotten that, but it was important that I remember.

My fingers slid to a stop, thinking about how Kace had walked me home the night before. It had started with him escorting me to my car, but his face had clouded when I told him that I didn't drive to the bar.

"You walk home at one in the morning?" he asked, quietly, but there was a thread of steel laced through his question.

Considering it had been at least a decade since anyone had given two shits about where I went or how I got home, I hadn't recognized that steel for what it was. That was what I got for dancing with trouble. "It's not far," I said, turning in the direction of my apartment.

"Not. Far."

That had triggered me, or at least I'd finally done the sensible thing and recognized the warning in Kace's tone.

"Well, I'll just . . . call you then?"

Silence.

I gave a painfully awkward wave. "Well . . . okay, bye."

One step. I got exactly one step before his fingers wrapped around my wrist and tugged me to a stop.

"Babe."

A beat. "Yeah?"

His voice softened. "You walk home?"

And somehow when his tone went gentler, mine firmed up. "I've been on my own for more than ten years, Kace. I know how to be smart and aware, and I know when I can walk three blocks safely."

He tugged my wrist, using the momentum to turn me so I was facing him again.

"There you are, gorgeous."

I rolled my eyes, and though his expression darkened, he didn't comment on the eye roll. Instead, he said, "Ten years."

Two words that weren't phrased as a question, but I knew he was asking one anyway, and it would be so easy to just blow him off, to give the standard non-answer that I always gave— small family, not close—and I didn't completely understand why, in this case, I didn't want to go that route.

I wanted Kace to know me. The real me.

"My parents died in a car accident when Hayden—my twin brother—and I were nineteen. I was at college, Hay, in the military." His fingers convulsed, and he reached for my other hand. "It was hard, especially because our family had just been us four, and with Hay in Afghanistan. I knew how dangerous it was there, and they couldn't get in contact with him after it happened. I thought . . ." My throat was so tight I could barely force the words out. "I thought I'd lost him, too." I sucked in a breath. "Then, later, I really did lose him."

Somehow, I found myself pressed into Kace's chest, the

steady thrum of his heartbeat against my ear. "I'm sorry, babe," he murmured, the words vibrating against my cheek. "That's a shit hand."

I stiffened. "He tried," I snapped, yanking myself out of Kace's arms and fully aware that the only reason I was able to do so was because he'd let me. "He tried to get better—"

The heat left me when I saw his face.

Because it wasn't pity in his expression, like I'd expected. Pity that I'd lost my parents and my brother had given up on me. Because it wasn't like that. Hayden had been sick and hurting and . . . we couldn't get him better.

Kace's face told me he understood that.

"I know," he murmured. "I know he tried to get better." He took my hand again, started walking me in the direction I'd pointed earlier. "With you in his life, he must have fought for it really hard."

If I'd thought my throat was tight before, now it had been burned to a crisp by a flamethrower, and I wasn't even going to think about how much my eyes stung. Instead, I just started walking beside Kace, blinking rapidly, breathing carefully, and leading the way to my apartment.

No surprise, he walked me up to my door.

But he didn't kiss me.

Instead, he cupped my cheek, touched his mouth to my forehead, and said, "Call me when you get up."

Then he took the keys from my hand and opened my door.

I was still reeling from sharing so much, from his reaction, from the way he made me feel *so fucking much,* when he nudged me inside, closing the door and ordering me to lock up.

I'd still been reeling as I'd done so then made my way to my laptop.

I hadn't heard my neighbor snoring, hadn't recognized the time passing by.

I'd sat my ass down and written and written and *written*.

I thought, I typed, I poured my soul into that computer.

And I did it until the sun came up.

I did it until I realized it was okay to share, that it was okay to not always be alone. I did it until I knew that somehow Kace was the one to make me feel that way, and I did it until I knew it wasn't just Kace and all his wonderfulness, that it was me, too, that *I* was tired of being alone.

And I wanted to try being *not* alone with Kace.

Then I closed my laptop, dropped myself into my bed fully dressed, and was asleep before my eyelids fully slid shut.

ELEVEN

Kace

SHE HADN'T CALLED.

Or texted.

Or Facebook friend requested me.

Fuck, I was old.

Also fuck, because I'd only made a profile on the site so I could stalk Brooke on her author page.

I'd given her my number so as not to pressure her, to go slowly and carefully, and for her to know the ball was in her court. That was totally fucking stupid. I knew that now. But I'd never expected her to let me in like she had the previous night, or earlier that same day, rather. If I'd known she would unlatch a piece of the armor she so diligently wore, I'd have gotten her number first thing.

I'd just expected that after six months of her barely making eye contact with me, it would take time to slip beneath that armor.

A whole lot of time.

And not to say that I was in all the way, but I'd gotten in a bit.

Which meant I'd expected a call within twenty-four hours. Or at least for Brooke to come into the bar during my shift that night. But she hadn't, and now I had two days off and was acting like a pussy-whipped motherfucker who was moping around waiting for his girl to phone.

Weak ass shit.

Sighing, I tossed the rag I was using to wipe down glasses into the dirty laundry bin, snagged my cell, and left the back room. As was my usual, I walked through the front of the bar, checking to make sure everything was ready for the crew to open at lunchtime and ensuring the front door was locked. Then armed the alarm, walked back down the hall and out the back door.

I double-checked that lock because I never knew what crazies were around then headed for my car, still moping, still sad and pathetic.

My phone buzzed.

Heart skipping a beat, I pulled it out of my pocket, but instead of it being an unknown number—read: Brooke—as I hoped, it was Heather, my new partner extraordinaire.

"Hey," I said, answering the call. "Still in Germany?"

"How'd you know?"

"Lunchtime."

"What?" she asked.

"You seem to enjoy calling me over salads."

A beat then, "Vegetables. Gross."

"Don't you know they make you strong?"

"I'm strong enough."

I plunked my ass into the driver's seat of the car. "I'm not saying I don't enjoy these late-night calls, but I've been on for ten hours, it's almost three am, and I haven't eaten yet."

"Right," Heather said, just as my phone buzzed, probably warning the battery was going to die since it was almost out of juice. "I'll get to the point. It's been a week since you signed the contract, and my stress level about Bobby's is a negative one million. Thanks."

I sucked in a breath, having not expected praise. "Oh. Heather—"

"Numbers are up, drama is down. I should have done this years ago." A beat. "You're the shit. Keep it up, and we'll talk new contract terms at the end of the year."

That was in less than six months.

What? "Heath—"

"You're kick ass. I knew it when I hired you, and I reward kick ass—"

"*Heather*."

"Yeah."

"You're the one who's the shit."

She laughed. "I agree with you."

I laughed, too. "Okay. We done here?"

I could sense her nodding, despite the fact that six thousand-ish miles separated us. "I'm done," she said. "I'll pop in to see you when I get back."

"Can't wait," I said dryly.

"I promise, I'll stick to the customer side of the bar."

"Considering that you dumped a tray full of pints on a couple the last time you tried to chip in and help, I'd say that is a good idea."

"One time," she teased as my phone buzzed again. "One time, a girl drops *one* thing."

"It was ten beers, if I recall correctly," I said. "But my phone's about to die, so I need to hang up and head home."

"Got it. Got to eat this healthy salad Clay has forced on me."

"Enjoy," I said to her snort and then we exchanged goodbyes.

I chucked my cell onto the passenger's seat, was starting to buckle in when I saw the screen flash on.

Not dying.

Two texts were on the screen.

Hey. I worked late last night and slept the day away. I can't believe it, but I just woke up. Are you at the bar still?

Then

Oh. This is Brooke btw.

It buzzed again as I read the messages.

Oh shoot. I probably caught you on your night off. Hope I didn't wake you. Talk to you another time.

Fuck that.

First thing I did was immediately save her number. The second thing I did was call that number. Unfortunately, I hadn't been joking with Heather about my battery being low. The moment I clicked the button to make the call, my cell died.

Cursing, I fumbled for my cord—which if I'd been smart would have been the first thing I did after hanging up with Heather—it wasn't there.

Which was when I remembered I'd taken it into my house the previous night.

"Idiot," I muttered. "I'm a total idiot."

Then I sighed and sat back into the seat. I should have—

Done a lot of things.

But tonight I had to be content with finally having Brooke's number, with having inched underneath that armor just a little further.

Or did I?

TWELVE

Brooke

I JUMPED when I heard it.

A soft *tap-tap*.

Immediately, my mind went full serial killer. I loved scary movies, so much so that I had a rotation of them on my streaming queue. A queue that was currently running in the background as I whipped up my favorite breakfast.

Three in the morning meant I was only a little early for bacon, eggs, and blueberry pancakes, right?

Right.

But then the tapping came again, and considering the tension was ramping up on my TV, the heroine and the murderer facing off and things about to go sideways, I nearly toppled my bowl of pancake batter.

Probably because the tap was more than a tap, and much closer to a pounding—*hehe*—my TV was set to loud, my neighbor was snoring blissfully away through it, and I had the kitchen fan running because the bacon was frying on the griddle pan.

I glanced toward the door just as another knock shook it in its panel.

Shit.

Had I woken someone?

I turned down the heat on the bacon, snagged the remote and paused the movie, then headed toward the door. Rising on tiptoe because I was a single girl, living alone, it was the middle of the night, and I wasn't stupid, I glanced through the peephole and felt my jaw drop open.

Um, what?

There wasn't an angry neighbor behind that wooden panel, or a police officer responding to a noise complaint as I'd half-expected.

It was . . . Kace.

Kace, whom I'd texted to no response (yes, I knew it was the middle of the night, no, that hadn't meant the lack of reply didn't hurt).

But still, it was gorgeous Kace, and I was . . .

Fucking hell. In my rattiest pajamas with bedhead the size of Texas and no bra.

"Brooke?" he called. "It's Kace."

"Uh . . . just a second!"

Shit. *Shit.*

My eyes darted around the room, noting the mismatched furniture covered in blankets and throw pillows, the paperbacks everywhere, my e-reader on the coffee table along with at least four dirty tea mugs. I had a pile of dirty laundry next to my stacked washer-dryer unit, dishes in the sink, and my bathroom was . . . questionable.

And I wasn't wearing a bra!

Another knock came. "Brooke? You okay? I smell something burning."

Shit!

My bacon. Not my bacon!

I reached for the lock, unlatched it, and threw open the door, getting all of one glimpse of Kace's gorgeous face before I spun in the opposite direction and ran to save my bacon, literally. A few pieces were nearing the edge of inedible, but I managed to salvage them and the rest, and by the time Kace made his way into my kitchen, I'd pulled all the strips off the griddle and set them to drain on a paper-towel-covered plate.

Then I flicked off the burner and turned to the man who'd invaded my apartment.

"Um, hi," I murmured.

Smooth.

But that inner eye roll stopped midway when I caught a glimpse of his face. It had gone molten and I swear, I felt his eyes drifting up from my toes, pausing on the threadbare short shorts I slept in before trailing further up to hesitate on my slouchy-sweater-but-no-bra-encased breasts.

"Hi," he whispered, eyes finally locking onto mine.

The look in them took my breath away.

"Kace?"

"I'm going to kiss you now."

My lungs froze.

"What?"

"You're in short shorts and not wearing a bra," he said, voice going husky. "So, I'm going to kiss you."

"Um . . ."

"Okay?"

Okay? Was he serious? I'd never been so attracted to a man, never fantasized about one so thoroughly for half a year, never touched one and felt sparks shoot down my fingertips. He was nice, thought I was pretty, was protective and a little possessive, and if I could hit pause on my feminist reel for a hot second in order to appreciate just how sexy that was—a man looking out for me, wanting me for me—because it was damned sexy. Plus, his kiss yesterday had blown my socks off. I wasn't about to turn the opportunity for another one of those down, definitely wasn't going to squander the kind of chemistry that was currently bubbling between us.

"Babe?"

I nodded. "You can kiss me," I murmured then held my breath.

I expected him to rush me, to slam me back against the counter, and plunder my mouth like a man possessed. Instead, he came near, but he did it slowly, prowling toward me, herding me backward until my spine hit the edge of the counter. He leaned close, my breath caught, his arm extended, and—

He reached passed me.

"Are these blueberries?"

My lungs hitched. My brain scrambled to figure out what in the ever-loving fuck he was talking about when Kace could have his mouth on mine, his tongue thrusting past my lips to tangle—

He picked up the bowl, brought it into the few inches between us.

My eyes flicked down and back up. "Yes." It was a whisper.

"I love blueberries," he murmured.

"Me, too." Another whisper.

"Hmm."

I felt that vibration of sound all the way to my toes. Okay, fine, that was a lie. It arrowed straight to my pussy and paused, causing heat to bloom and moisture to pool.

Kace studied the bowl for an interminable moment before plucking out one round berry and setting the rest aside. He brought it up to his lips, and I saw a flash of white as his teeth came down and bit it in half.

I jolted, feeling those teeth on my clit as realistically as if he'd been between my thighs.

He finished chewing, and his mouth curved. But I barely noticed. My gaze was on his hand. He was carefully running the remaining half of the berry between his finger, squeezing gently so the juice was dripping out and coating the tips. Then he brought them up to his mouth and sucked them clean.

My mind blanked out.

Another berry found its way into his hand, my brain too hazy to process him reaching for the bowl or conjuring it out of who knew where, because this time he brought it to my lips, encouraging me to take a bite.

So, I did.

The flavor exploded in my mouth, tart chased by sweet, juice coating my tongue as I chewed and swallowed.

"Good?" he asked.

I nibbled the corner of my mouth and nodded.

Blue eyes went hotter. "I promised that the next time I saw you do that"—he nodded toward my bottom lip—"I was going to take a bite out of that pretty mouth." Before I could fully process what he'd said, Kace had leaned down, nipped at my lips, then straightened, cocky grin in place.

I lifted my hand to my mouth, touched the stinging corner, and yet it didn't hurt exactly. More like, it was pulsing, nerves firing, suddenly desperate for more than a flash of teeth.

Kace must have read that because he snagged my wrist, tugged my hand away, and then brought his fingertips up and brushed them across my lips.

Or painted.

Because they were dripping in sticky blueberry juice that he dragged across my mouth. "I fucking love blueberries," he muttered, and *then* he kissed me.

I was beyond turned on. I was trembling, knees shaky, pussy clenching, body on fire, and so, when his mouth finally touched mine, I exploded into action. My hands slid into his hair, weaving tightly the same time I jumped and wrapped my thighs around his waist. He caught me, hands on my ass, pressing me into the counter, grinding the length of his erection against my center. As all of that was happening, his mouth was working, his tongue thrusting deep and in time to the movements of his hips.

It was rough. It was wet. It was raunchy.

And it was by far the hottest kiss of my life.

But eventually my lungs demanded oxygen, and so, I had to pull away. Kace released my mouth when I tugged lightly at his hair, his hot, rapid breaths puffing against my lips, his eyes darkened to navy, his palms still cupping my ass.

Then one of his fingers moved, and I shuddered.

"You know you have a hole here?"

"Wh-what?"

His calloused fingertip brushed against my bare skin. "You've got a hole"—another brush, this time lower and more inside—"here."

"I do?"

He bent, tongue tracing across my collarbone that was exposed by my loose sweatshirt. "No panties. No bra. Holes showing off that gorgeous ass and a shirt that's about to fall off." His eyes came up to meet mine. "You're trying to kill me."

"I'm not trying to do anything," I grumbled and shoved at his chest, but he didn't budge. "You barged in here and got all up in my blueberries."

He lifted a brow. "I thought you loved blueberries."

"Exactly," I said. "But I don't love to share."

A grin. "I think I can make it up to you."

I crossed my arms.

His eyes flicked down. "Not helping me with your no bra situation, babe."

I huffed. "You gonna put me down?"

Kace's lips pressed together, head tilting as he considered that. "Will you make me pancakes if I do?"

Now, it was my chance to consider.

But it turned out that I should have considered longer because the next words that came out of my mouth were—

"I'll make you pancakes, if you go down on me."

THIRTEEN

Kace

I STARED DOWN AT BROOKE, unable to believe the words that just came out of her pretty, little mouth.

Though, she hadn't been showing me much shy over the last few days. I'd seen the fire underneath that armor, had felt the heat of her lips and body against mine. And I'd read some of her books. Shy might be the surface, but shy wasn't what was inside.

"Babe," I murmured.

She nibbled on the corner of her mouth again, and I felt that flash of teeth along my cock.

"*Babe.*"

A warning this time. A reminder of what that did to me.

Her lip slid free, glistening slightly, and *fuck* that was just as bad.

"Look at me."

Emerald eyes rose to meet mine, and the heat in them was palpable. She wanted my mouth on her. *I* wanted that, too. Fuck yes, I did. I'd just needed to see the confirmation in her face, didn't want to jump too fast when we were just getting started—

Her cheeks flushed red, and those pretty eyes started to turn away.

Yeah, that wasn't happening.

I pushed the bowl of blueberries to the side, shoved the pathetic excuse for shorts she was wearing down, and plunked her onto the edge of the counter.

She gasped, probably from the cold of the tile hitting her ass, but I didn't give her time to focus on that. I dropped to my knees, yanked her shorts the rest of the way off, and shoved myself between her thighs. Then I spread her wide and dove into her pussy.

Normally, I'd go slow, trying to learn every single thing she liked, every spot that made her squirm and moan, but consciously aware of it or not, we'd both had six months of foreplay. Which meant she was dripping wet and the first touch of my tongue against her clit made her scream, grip my head with both hands, and start riding my mouth.

So there wasn't time for tricks or finesse or fancy techniques.

I firmed my tongue, kept it moving, and let her do her thing.

And she did it incredibly well, finding a rhythm that I matched, savoring the sweetness of her against my tongue, thinking that my woman fucking my face was the hottest experience of my life.

Her hands tightened in my hair and she let out a keening moan, but her motions started to falter, so I took over. She was hovering on the edge, and I gripped her hips, moved closer, flicking my tongue harder and faster until her head fell forward, and she stiffened, another moan escaping her lips, but this was one of release instead of desperation.

I guided her down, easing up on her clit, slowing my movements until she went limp.

Carefully, I untangled her fingers and reached for her shorts, slipping them over her ankles then lifting her off the counter to tug them up and over her hips.

"Thanks," she murmured, forehead dropping to my chest.

"For the orgasm or the shorts?"

A huff of laughter. "You're a troublemaker, aren't you?"

I grinned. "Only in my day job."

She shook her head then gasped when I scooped her up into my arms. "I owe you pancakes," she said.

I carried her to the couch, grabbed one of the hundred blankets tossed over it, and tucked it around her. But when I saw what was printed on it, I grinned. "*Book Me Harder*?" I asked.

Her cheeks went pink again. "One of my readers sent it to me." She started to slide it off, but I tugged it back in place. "Pancakes, remember?"

"I remember," I told her. "I'll make them."

She nibbled at her lip, and I took advantage of her cuteness to steal another kiss. "Fuck, babe. Makes me hard when you do that."

More pink, but her emerald eyes flashed with fire. "Can I feel the evidence of that?"

My brow lifted. "Who's the troublemaker now?"

Her grin took my breath away, but I forced myself to turn for the kitchen, to scoop up the bowl of pancake batter and start heating up the griddle. I wasn't a great cook, but I could do breakfast.

"There enough for two here? Or should I make more batter?"

Silence.

I rotated to face her. "Babe?"

"Are you seriously going to make me pancakes?" she asked. "I mean I pro—"

"I don't need any motivation to go down on you, babe," I said. "I've been dreaming about it for six months. And I know I showed up in the middle of the night, but I didn't exactly plan on coming here for a booty call. I came because my cell died before I could text you back and I was close by, so it was easy to walk a few blocks. Though I did see some dude walking around in his underwear, and that was very confusing because he said he was on vacation, and why you'd walk around in your underwear because you're on vacation, let alone be doing it in the middle of the night, I don't know." I shrugged. "Anyway, my point is that I came because you texted and because I think we have something special, but that the special is new and unexplored, so I came to ask you to go out to dinner with me tomorrow."

Spinning, I turned back to the bowl, decided there was enough batter for two, and started ladling it on the now-hot griddle.

"Kace?"

"Yeah?" I kept my focus on the pancakes.

"I was going to make eggs, too."

I shook my head, but I was grinning. "Quiet, but definitely a troublemaker." I grabbed the spatula off the counter and began flipping. "But turns out, I make great scrambled eggs."

FOURTEEN

Brooke

I WAS SITTING NEXT to Kace, a plate of pancakes, bacon, and eggs balanced on my lap, *Scream* playing in the background because it turned out he liked scary movies, too.

Well actually, he'd said, "I'm more of an action man, but I can get behind horror films, too."

And then I'd snorted because the only thing I could focus on was *action* and *getting behind,* and I might be a grown woman, but I also had never grown out of my dirty mind. Probably because I got to write all the dirty jokes I wanted in my books and partly because what was life without a few innuendos?

Kace had taken one look at my face, grinned again—I really, *really* liked his smile—and handed me my plate. Then he'd leaned down and nipped my jaw, whispering in my ear, "Troublemaker."

I liked that.

Liked that somehow I could be me when I was with Kace.

Absently, I picked up the remote and hit fast-forward. For

some reason, the bathroom scene where the killer comes out and attacks the girl at the mirror had always freaked me out. So, I skipped it.

Same with the dog scene in *I Am Legend*. I couldn't do it, so I skipped ahead.

I hit play, tossed the remote down, and started shoveling in pancakes again. Probably, I should have made an effort to eat slowly or daintily or something, but I was cuddled in a blanket in ratty pjs with a movie from my child—well, teenage—hood on the TV.

This wasn't time for fancy.

It was time to hang out. With Kace. Who—whoops—was staring at me like I'd grown two heads?

"Whatcha doing?" he asked carefully.

I shrugged. "Scene freaks me out."

His head tilted to the side and he paused, his fork with a square of blueberry pancake still speared on it three inches from his mouth. "So, let me get this straight," he said and shoved it into his mouth, quickly chewing and swallowing before he moved on. "You love scary movies, but when you watch them, you fast-forward through all the scary parts."

I wrinkled my nose. "Not *all* the scary parts," I muttered. "Just the ones that are really bad."

He stared at me for a good ten seconds. Then his lips started twitching, warmth sunk into his eyes, and he burst out laughing. "Holy shit, babe," he said and started back in on the pancakes.

I set my plate on the table with a *thunk*. "Don't laugh at me."

Instant quiet.

"Babe." He stopped, stared at me, considering. "I'm not laughing at you."

"Heard that before," I said with a scoff and stood, not one hundred percent sure why I was pissed off, why I was pushing this. But . . . I hardly knew the man and he was in my apartment, *laughing* at me and—

"You should go." I took a step, intending to show him the front door.

But I'd forgotten about the blanket and so that single step was enough for me to eat it. The fleece tangled around my ankles, I lost my balance, and tipped toward the coffee table, arms flailing for purchase.

I heard Kace grunt, but I was more concerned with the oak coming straight at my forehead.

Except, it didn't come.

Warm hands grabbed my shoulders, and I was yanked backward.

I'd been on my feet. Now I was in Kace's lap.

"Babe," he murmured.

I closed my eyes, unable to look at him. "I think you should go," I said again.

More silence. But this time it was trailed by a sigh. "You really want me to go, I'll leave, but I'm not going until I've said this."

My shoulders tightened. I knew what was coming, what he'd realized. That we were too different, on completely alternate scales. I'd thought I could be all self-loving and get over the disparity between us, between his absolute beauty and my normalness, but I couldn't because I knew that one day he wouldn't look at my quirks as amusing little trifles, as cute little things that Brooke did. One day he'd resent my books, me brushing him off when I was on deadline, me living in a fictional world instead of the real one. And someday, he'd want me to wear something sexy when I *wasn't* sexy. I was T-shirts and scrunchies and mom jeans. The closest thing approaching sexy I had were some false lashes in my makeup drawer that I'd nearly managed to glue to my cheek instead of my eye, where they belonged.

He might think *I* was great now.

But that wouldn't last.

It *never* lasted.

"I don't know why you're doing this."

"Look at me." Kace's palm cupped my cheek then slid into my hair, tilting my head so when I opened my eyes, I could see straight into this. "You don't see yourself clearly. You hide—"

I stiffened and tried to pull away, but he simply wrapped an arm around my waist and kept me in place.

"You hide," he said again. "Hide your beauty and your sense of humor. I don't know why you're hiding, but I do know that you gave me—a guy who hasn't had much good in his life—a glimpse of what's inside of you six months ago when you smiled up at me for refilling your glass. That smile was pure, and it was sweet, and I didn't forget it, babe. I kept making it my mission to get that smile, until you felt comfortable enough to show me more of you."

His fingers tugged lightly at my hair. "I saw you with Brent, saw how *he* was with you, and I knew he saw the same. So, I know I jumped from cautious to warp speed real fast, but I also knew that if I didn't, I'd miss out on the opportunity to get to know you." A beat. "And a guy like me, a guy who grew up in the system, who joined the military because it was the only way out of shit, a guy who had to deal with the fallout of serving because while it's noble shit, it still leaves a fuck-ton of demons behind. Also, being a guy who never knew sweet and silly and blushes actually existed . . . for him, for *me*, I knew I needed to grab on to the chance to know that."

He bent, kissed me on the forehead, and gently shifted so he could slip out from under me.

I couldn't move because his words were circling through my head, absolutely pounding through my brain.

Kace scooped up the plates, put them in the sink, then headed for the front door.

"I know I got in that gorgeous mind of yours, babe, but I'm gonna need you to get up at least to lock the door."

I couldn't move, didn't know how to move.

But apparently my lips did because—

"Spare key is in the drawer next to the oven. Daisy keychain."

A beat of quiet then, "You like daisies?"

"My favorite flower."

"I'm off tonight," he said. "I'll bring you some."

I still didn't move, was still frozen to the couch cushions, but I did hear his footsteps moving across the floor, heard the drawer open, and the contents move as he retrieved the key. My heart was pounding, I was sweating, my throat was constricted impossibly tight.

Just before he reached the door, I managed to squeeze out, "I'll cook."

His feet paused. "Babe," he murmured.

Then the door closed.

A second later the lock clicked.

A second after that the tears came.

I just couldn't figure out if they were happy or sad.

* * *

An hour later, I'd showered, thrown sweats and a shirt on, and had my phone in my hand. I wanted to call Hay, to talk to my twin so desperately about Kace, but he was gone, and I was alone and . . . maybe I wasn't quite as alone as I'd previously thought.

Sucking in a breath, I hit the call button on my cell.

One ring. Two. Three. Four.

But just before I was going to hang up, Brent answered, voice slightly roughened with sleep. "Brookie girl, you okay darlin'?"

And cue more tears.

There was rustling and a sigh.

"Not okay," he muttered.

"I'm fine," I said quickly, suddenly feeling stupid for calling him. "I'm sorry, I shouldn't have—"

"Coffee. Place on the corner near the bar. Thirty minutes."

"I—"

"Darlin'. Thirty minutes."

Nodding, even though he couldn't see me, I sniffed again. "Okay."

He hung up.

I picked up my laptop—because it was highly effective as a shield and because I could never resist the opportunity to get a few words on the page—decided to head down to the shop early. Maybe I could puzzle myself out so Brent and I could catch up without me looking like a drama queen who didn't know her own head.

Except, I *didn't* know my own head.

After grabbing a jacket and my trusty backpack, I headed for the door.

Five minutes later I was at the coffee shop, five minutes after that an espresso had cleared my head.

Kind of.

And ten minutes after that, Brent walked in.

He didn't spot me then go to the counter to order a coffee. He saw me and came straight over, dragging a chair so he was sitting very close to me, close enough that his dark eyes delved into mine.

After a moment, he sat back and sighed. "So, I don't have to kill him then."

My brows drew down. I couldn't tell if he was relieved or disappointed. "What—?"

He stood and went to the counter, ordering a black coffee in a place that specialized in every sort of fancy drink imaginable. I knew, because I imagined a lot and thus had tried most of the menu.

But since a black coffee didn't take long, he was back sitting at my table in just a few moments.

Sitting and staring.

I knew this trick—silently outwaiting a conversational partner—because Hayden had often used it with me. Often because it worked well.

This time was no different.

"I'm scared."

Nary a beat before, "This is about Steven."

"This *isn't* about Steven."

"You've got a good man interested and you're scared."

Scared of diving in, scared of what might happen if I didn't. But that still didn't mean it had anything to do with my ex.

"Steven."

I sighed and sat back in my chair. "I don't see how they're even remotely the same, even if I *was* still hung up on Steven."

He took a sip of his manly black coffee. "They're not the same. Not even close. And I didn't say that you were still hung up on Steven, just that this was about your past with your ex."

"I—"

"He was all charm and surface, darlin'. All fluff without substance. Hayden didn't think he was going to stick, even before everything went down."

My breath caught. "Hayden didn't like him?"

Brent's face softened. "Hayden wasn't ever going to like the man who took his sister away, but he also knew that Steven wasn't right for you."

"Oh."

His fingers rested on my knee. "He knew you deserved the fairy tale, darlin'. The happy ending you write about in your books. Steven, for all his smoothness, wasn't going to be that man for you, and your brother knew that." He smiled. "But he also knew that if you were happy, he wasn't going to mess it up, no matter if he thought the guy wasn't good enough."

I sniffed. "Really?"

Brent nodded. "Really."

"Steven turned out to be an asshole," I said. "So, Hay was right."

Brent laughed. "Believe me, he would have loved to agree with you about that." Another sip from his cup before his eyes sobered. "But for what it's worth, I wouldn't have backed off from taking my shot at seeing if you and I fit"—my breath caught because I thought if Kace wasn't in the picture that Brent and I might have fit very well—"for anyone aside from Kace. He's a good guy. Substance *and* smooth." He grinned. "Kind of like me."

My lips twitched. "And modest, too."

But Brent's words wove their way into my heart, soothing the frightened, trembling organ. I knew what he said was the truth, even if I didn't want to admit it. Steven hadn't been the greatest boyfriend, and he'd been an even shittier fiancée leaving me when he had. But the reason Kace scared me so much was because I knew deep down that he wasn't like Steven.

So I'd tried to push him away, even though I wanted him desperately.

And when that hadn't worked, I'd started trying to find reasons to run back into my safe bubble and hide.

But I didn't want to hide any longer.

I wanted Kace.

Now, I just had to be brave enough to go for it.

I blinked, saw that Brent was just quietly sipping his coffee as I puzzled out my head, and I realized I'd gained two really important things in the last week—a potential future and a link to my past.

I hadn't realized how much I'd wanted both.

I also decided I was going to keep them. Both.

Brent smiled at me. "Sorted?"

I bit my lip because my brother had always said that to me, and then I put down my cup and reached over to hug him. "Thank you," I murmured.

"Anytime, darlin'. Anytime."

And then with my future blossoming ahead of me, I spent the next hour remembering many of the good parts of my past that I'd forgotten.

There was hysterical laughter over a story of Hayden and Brent's military days, a little snorting at my brother's lack of game with the ladies, some sniffing when we talked about how hard it was to lose him. But we mostly focused on the good times —the inside jokes, the care packages, the stinky socks, and Hay's horrifying affinity for liking all things clown.

Brent walked me home, telling me all about the places he'd been in the years since we'd seen one another, and we both smiled when thinking about how despite all that, we'd still ended up in the same town.

He paused at my door. "I'd say, don't be a stranger, but I don't think Kace is going to let that happen anyway."

I smiled. "I don't think *I'm* going to let that happen."

One finger traced my jaw, his lips curved. "I don't think so, either. Oh, Brooke?" he said when I'd turned away and started to unlock my door. "Just remember that Kace might be able to charm every female who walks over to the bar, but *you're* the only one I've ever seen that makes him mess up drink orders and lose his cool."

"I—"

"It's a good way to get more tips, but that's *all* it is."

"I—"

"You're different. You're *important*." He scowled. "And he saw that before I did."

"Brent—"

He nudged me inside and closed the door. "See you soon, darlin'."

I sighed, locked up, and called my goodbyes.

FIFTEEN

Kace

I KNOCKED on the door later that same evening, unaccountably nervous, but also cautiously optimistic.

Probably because I'd never told a woman, even in the vaguest of terms that I'd given to Brooke hours before, about my upbringing. Probably because no woman had ever been important enough for me to tell her jackshit about me. I kept the past locked down where it belonged, and I kept my relationships light.

But Brooke meant more to me than my secrets.

Scary as fuck, but the truth.

I loved how when she pulled her ponytail up in the bar, it always ended up slightly askew, as though she couldn't bear to tear her fingers away from her keyboard long enough to make it perfectly straight.

I loved how she took a sip of every fresh Diet Coke I brought her then promptly forgot about it, as she got lost in her characters.

I loved that she wore T-shirts and jeans and Chucks and not heels and slinky dresses.

I loved . . . her.

It made no sense. I'd never been the type of man to believe in happily ever afters or love at first sight.

But Brooke made me think those were real.

She might write about fictional characters finding their own happiness, but she'd been integral in helping me find the hope that I could actually get mine.

For a guy with no family, that was huge.

Now, I just had to convince her to take a chance on me.

I knocked on the door, not certain that the key she'd given me to lock up hours before also meant I had enter-at-will access. I didn't want to be presumptuous, but I also didn't want to give her the opportunity to take the key back.

Footsteps approached, and I prepared myself for the emotional assault that was Brooke.

Then I didn't have time to prepare because the door was open, she was there, the assault was complete, and my breath had been stolen. Thoroughly, absolutely stolen. How she thought she wasn't beautiful was insanity, and I made a mental note then and there that I'd make it my life's mission to make her understand how truly perfect she was.

"Hi," she murmured, hand on the doorjamb, shy smile that didn't quite reach her eyes on her face. And those eyes were ringed with red.

Fuck. She'd been crying.

I should offer to leave, be a good man and just leave her alone.

But I wasn't a good man.

I was selfish, and Brooke was the best thing I'd ever had in my life, and I wasn't going to give her up.

"Hi," I said gently and handed her the bouquet because it

turned out I could be the type of man to buy her flowers. "It smells good in here."

"Thank you. They're beautiful." She nodded. "My mom's lasagna recipe."

We stood there, staring at each other until I brushed a finger along her jaw. "Can I come in?"

There was that blush I liked so much, but she nodded and stepped back. "Of course," she said, rushing through the words. "I'm sorry, it's been a day."

I went inside and closed the door then just decided we needed to get this shit out there and over with. "Because of me?"

Teeth on the corner of her mouth.

"Babe."

Those teeth disappeared, and she sucked in a breath. "Yes. Because of you."

My gut sank.

"But not why you think."

The sinking stopped.

"Babe."

She took my hand, tugged me to the couch. "Stop hovering over me and come here," she murmured. "I need to talk to you."

"Yeah." It was a mutter. "I've got some things to say to you as well."

Her face clouded, worry evident. But that worry was enough to settle my own because there wouldn't be worry if she didn't care or was wanting me to keep my distance.

"Babe." Her eyes flashed up. "It's not the way you think."

Warmth.

Relief.

Fuck, I loved this woman.

Then she nodded, and still holding my hand, sat on the couch. "Okay," she breathed. "You know about my family. You know that I've been alone for a long time. But"—I decided that I didn't like that *but*, not at all—"when I lost Hayden, I wasn't all alone." A beat. "I was engaged."

I didn't like that. Not at all. However, since a *was* was involved, I was okay, but because there *was* a was involved and it had left that expression on her face, then I decided I *really* didn't like the fact that she'd worn another man's ring.

"He didn't stick," she said. "For my own reasons, but mostly because of him saying it was me."

Fucking asshole.

"Yeah," she said. "He was."

I didn't realize I'd said that aloud, though that didn't make it any less true. "Babe," I said. "How soon after you lost your brother?"

A sigh. "Three weeks."

I shot to my feet. "Are you *fucking* kidding me?"

Her lips curved slightly. "Nope. It was a good thing, though." She stopped when her eyes hit mine, probably because in that moment, I was thinking how much I wanted to kill the bastard. "No, really, it was."

"I think, based on the fact that I left you hours ago and your eyes are red because you've been crying all day, that it wasn't a good thing."

Brooke's free hand found my face. "Baby."

I mock-glared. "So, I can't call you baby, but you can call *me* that?"

She grinned. "I let babe slide, didn't I?"

Turning my head, I pressed a kiss to her palm. "Yes, you did," I said. "I've been meaning to ask you, *why* is that?"

Red-hot cheeks.

"Babe."

Her eyes dropped to the couch. "I should check on the lasagna," she said and tried to stand.

Like I was going to let that slide.

"*Babe*," I said, snagging her waist and tugging her back into my lap.

"It's not important."

"By your reaction, I'd say it's pretty damned important."

She was in my lap and actively squirming to get away, which meant that my body had what one might term as a typical reaction. Meaning her ass was rubbing against my dick and my dick got hard.

Surprise. That was nature at work.

But I knew the moment she felt it because she froze . . . and then she began rubbing in a completely different way. Which meant I had to clamp my arm around her waist, and that was both heaven and hell. Heaven because her ass was in my lap and she was still wiggling. Hell because she wasn't naked while doing said wiggling.

"Babe," I growled and nipped her throat. It was there, and it smelled like the flowers I'd brought her . . . and it was part of Brooke, my mouth was close, and it was there.

She shivered and I swear to God, the sound she made in the back of her throat was the sexiest thing I'd ever heard.

"It . . . doesn't"—I trailed my tongue up her throat—"ah. Baby— I—"

"Why is babe okay, but nothing else?"

"It doesn't—"

"It does." I nipped again.

"It—"

My mouth latched on, sucking softly, using my teeth, soothing with my tongue. "Babe."

"Fine," she panted. "Babe is okay because I've never heard you use it with another woman."

That froze me. "What?"

"You call every woman who comes into the bar baby or

sweetheart or *honey*," she muttered, and I found I liked that she sounded grumpy.

"I'm fairly certain that I've never called any other woman sugar pie."

Pink cheeks again. "Okay, fine, that was mostly out of spite."

"Mostly?" I teased. "So, should I add it back into my endearment repertoire?"

"Not if you want to live." A hesitation then, "Brent told me you weren't the player I thought. I—uh . . . and I guess this is the point where I admit that Steven did factor into this, at least slightly. He used all of those endearments"—a flash of a smile—"sugar pie, aside. But he didn't really mean them either, you know? It was just something superficial." Her voice dropped. "I didn't want to be superficial, even in the beginning."

"Babe–"

"But Brent pointed that out, and I thought it over and I get that's not you. I also get that you using those endearments is just part of your bar persona in a way, and that using them gets you guys more tips." She shrugged, lips curving again. "I'm not going to get upset over something that gets you more tips."

This woman.

My heart pounded and I wanted to let her know how much her words meant to me, but I also didn't want to make the moment heavy again. Not when she was smiling. Still, Brent was right. Sometimes I didn't even think about the fact that I was using them. I'd have to be more careful.

Fewer tips meant nothing, if Brooke was happy.

"Hmm. Sugar pie does have a nice ring to it," I teased, tapping my finger to my lips. She elbowed me. Hard. "*Kidding.* But just saying, maybe babe is my key to even more tips. *Oof.*" Another elbow that had me wincing. "Okay, so babe is yours, but just know you have free rein to call me whatever you want."

"How about cocky bastard?" she asked, eyes flashing, but mouth curving.

I laughed. "If it allows the word cock to cross your lips, then yes."

A roll of her eyes, but her lips were twitching. "I'll take babe."

"How magnanimous. Now, back to the ex and the reason you were crying."

I'd been wrong earlier. Brooke stopping her fight to get free from me and slumped back against my chest, her head nuzzling close until it was tucked under my chin was the best feeling in the world. I'd had girls cuddle up to me before, obviously. But not like this, not like she was seeking my touch because it somehow comforted her or gave her the strength to lay it out there.

Though, I was probably imagining a lot of that, still I fucking loved her tucked close, and I'd take that any day of the week.

"Babe."

"Brooke," she muttered.

I smirked. *"Babe."*

Her sigh was warm against my throat. "You sure you want this drama out there? I was trying to keep our first date light."

"This isn't our first date."

She frowned, leaned back. "I mean, I know I gave it up a bit last night, er, earlier today, but I think I'd remember going on a date with you, Kace."

"You wore a green hoodie with a book embroidered over your heart. You had your laptop, though there were a few less stickers on its case, and I refilled your glass three times with Diet Coke, even though you only took a total of four sips from them."

"I—"

"Two from the first, none from the second, two from the

third." I touched her nose. "Then you closed your computer, smiled up at me with those lush lips and pink cheeks, and you asked for a Rum and Coke. *That* was the only drink you finished."

"I—"

"Then you nibbled on the corner of your mouth—like you're doing now—and I wanted to kiss you as much then as I do now."

She released her bottom lip along with a shuddering breath. "Why didn't you? Why *don't* you?"

"First," I said, tracing my thumb over the oft-injured spot on her mouth, "I didn't want to get arrested for assaulting a woman I'd shared less than twenty words with. And second . . . chemistry isn't our issue, babe. But we jumped over a bunch of getting-to-know-you steps, and that means I need to make sure we don't keep skipping over important stuff."

"What if I said it wasn't important?"

"An ex who left you three weeks after you lost your twin and who still makes you cry—"

"Steven didn't make me cry."

Steven. Figured. Biggest asshole growing up at my school was a Steven.

I lifted a brow.

Brooke rolled her eyes. "I'm going to say this once and then we're done with it, okay?"

Since I wasn't going to agree with that bit of nonsense—we'd talk shit out as often as it was necessary—I just cupped her cheek. "Tell me."

"I got together with Steven after my parents died. Hay never liked him, said he treated me like shit instead of glass, but he was there and into me and . . ." A sigh. "I was a different person with him and not a good one. In fact, I actually had stopped writing because he didn't like the time it took away from him. So in the end, it was a good thing that I got dumped. It gave me the strength to get back to myself."

"Still say he's an asshole," I muttered.

She laughed. "I'm not going to argue with that."

"Tears."

"Dog to a bone, aren't you?"

"When it's something I care about, then yes."

Her face softened, and I decided in my mental tally of great things that were Brooke, *this* was the best. Her looking at me like that, letting me in a little deeper, fucking nirvana.

"I was crying because it was the first time I opened my mom's cookbook since she died."

Oh.

Oh.

Fuck, this woman undid me

"I don't know what we have," she said, voice soft. "But I've spent a lot of time over the last couple of days thinking about it. I obviously want to jump your bones, but it's more than that. Maybe it's the silent six months of dating"—her small smile made my heart skip a beat—"or maybe it's just that this thing between us is special—"

"It is."

"Regardless, I like you a lot, Kace. Probably more than is smart or prudent, but there it is." A shrug. "I made my mom's lasagna because I wanted to impress you and also because it's incredible and people always go back for seconds, so I knew I'd keep you at the table to try and make up for a few of the, as you call them, getting-ahead-of-ourselves steps."

My pulse pounded because she got it, because she was right there with me.

And because of that, I knew we'd had enough of the heavy.

So I just met her eyes, gave her a soft, "Thank you," and then stood so we could both find our feet.

"I'll set the table," I told her. "You check on that delicious-smelling lasagna."

She nodded and started for the kitchen then paused, reaching down to pick up a blanket that had fallen to the floor during her struggles. "Kace?"

"Hmm?"

Brooke glanced back, totally caught me staring at her ass, but fuck, her butt looked amazing in those tight jeans.

"Baby?"

I got my shit together and forced my gaze up.

She was smiling. "Dishes are in the cabinet next to the sink."

"On it."

I tugged the end of her ponytail as I strode by, rubbing the silken ruby strands between my fingers. "Pretty."

"Charmer."

"I try."

"Try is the operative word."

I burst out laughing. Then Brooke bent to check on the pan of lasagna in the oven, and I got busted staring at her ass again.

But as I'd already established, it was a fantastic ass.

So totally worth it.

"Kace?"

I forced my eyes up.

"I don't trust easily." A brief hesitation. "Current company aside."

My heart skipped a beat. "I know, babe. Which is why we're going to tread carefully moving forward. Okay?"

Her smile was soft. "More than okay. That sounds perfect."

SIXTEEN

Brooke

I SKIPPED into the bar two days later, having spent the last two evenings with Kace.

The first, we'd devoured the lasagna, then hunkered down on the couch and binged watched Marvel movies. And this time, there was no fast-forwarding through the scary bits, mostly because there weren't any scary bits. Perilous, exciting, funny, and sometimes tear-inducing, but not frightening. They didn't completely fill my horror void, but sitting cuddled up next to Kace as he'd stroked his fingers through my ponytail over and over again had filled a different one.

I felt lighter than I had in years, almost buoyant. I'd laid it all on him, and he hadn't shied away, hadn't blinked, hadn't run.

So, there were butterflies in my tummy, heat in my—cough —but most importantly, I didn't feel as though I were waiting for the other shoe to drop.

The second night, Kace took me out to dinner.

And not at three in the morning, though it was nice that he was as much of a night owl as I was.

We'd gone into the city and hit Little Italy, devouring arancini and handmade pasta, gorging ourselves on rolls, then he'd walked me to my door, laid a kiss on me that had me seeing stars, and whispered, "I really like the dress," before shutting me safely in my apartment.

I'd been disappointed to say the least. I'd pulled out the one thing that wasn't jeans and T-shirts in my closet. I'd even worn fancy shoes and makeup. But he hadn't come in.

My cell had buzzed two seconds after the lock engaged.

You deserve someone who treads carefully with you.

The exhale slipping through my lips was shaky. And that was before the next text.

I'll be dreaming about that glimpse of black lace I saw when the wind lifted your skirt.

I'd slipped off my shoes, headed into my bedroom to change into my pajamas, and then my phone had vibrated again.

But not as much as you in those thin ass shorts you're probably slipping into right now.

Fire.

The man was fire, and I was going up in flames while I was trying to remind myself that he was being sweet at slowing the physical stuff down, as well as smart because we should get to know each other more.

But I didn't want to.

I wanted my shorts on the floor and his mouth on me again.

Then I wanted the hard length that I'd been lucky enough to feel a few times to slip inside and show me everything I'd been imagining he could do with it. And considering the way he'd used his tongue on me, I'd expanded on my imaginings a whole hell of a lot.

I decided to ponder on that.

Not so much the imaginings, as where I saw things going with Kace and if I needed to tread carefully or if, for the first time in my life, I was ready to leap in with both feet and figure out the rest later.

I had been leaning toward the latter after that second night, but the text from Kace that morning—well, more early afternoon since I'd managed to squeeze in a few words before my chainsawing neighbor had messed with my mojo and the words had stopped flowing.

I'd sent Kace a text forgetting the time, just before I'd gone to bed, telling him goodnight.

Then I'd woken up to:

Hope your characters treated you right, babe. But if you're going to write me into more books, then you have to do it with that sweet ass on a stool in my bar.

Curious, I'd replied.

Why?

A buzz.

Because then I get your smiles for refilling drinks you don't actually drink.

I'd laughed, stretched, and sent back a response.

Lies. But anyway, I need to change out of these shorts and do a few errands. Before I go, I have a very serious question for you.

My cell went off.

Scary shit, babe. But shoot.

I wrinkled my nose, strangely bummed that he hadn't commented on my mention of shorts, but dutifully went on with my line of questioning.

Pumpkin or chocolate?

Silence then,

Might as well break out the cat of nine making me choose between those.

I would have been lying if I'd said my heart wasn't fluttering.

Then how about pumpkin AND chocolate?

His reply came in seconds.

I'd say you're the perfect woman for me.

I was still catching my breath from that particular comment (dangerous, charming, and fucking the best ever) when my cell vibrated again.

Also, no fair about the shorts if I can't be there to see you in them.

I grinned.

Goodbye, Kace. See you tonight.

The next buzzes came in rapid succession.

Fuck. You're still wearing them.

Maybe.

Killing me.

See you tonight.

Bye, babe.

Bye.

I'd flopped back on my bed, lips curved, still buoyant, still fluttering, but . . . no longer nervous. I was all in. Kace and I might end with heartbreak, but I knew I couldn't miss the glorious ride along the way.

So I'd gotten up, showered, and hit the grocery store. I'd made him awesome pumpkin bread with chocolate chunks and a caramel crumble (from my mom's cookbook, and this time I didn't cry) and did my weekly duty with the laundry pile in the hallway. Then because I'd started my chores in the early afternoon and now it was early evening and Kace would be at the bar, I gathered my stuff and hoofed it the few blocks over.

I'd also worn the black lace.

It was just under my mom jeans and Baby Yoda T-shirt.

Because I was plying him with pumpkin and chocolate and tempting him (hopefully) with the lace.

Now it was smack dab in the middle of dinnertime, and the bar was packed. I hesitated at the door, suddenly nervous because so much had changed since the last time I'd been in. But the changes were good, so I lifted my chin and waded my way through the throngs of people. Brent wasn't on, which I thought was a good thing since I was still finding my footing with this taking chances and diving headfirst thing and didn't need my brother's friend keeping an eye on me.

I also didn't need him antagonizing Kace.

I *did* need to take him out to dinner as I'd previously promised and catch up.

Tonight, however, was about Kace and me and pumpkin bread and black lace. I slipped between a gabbing group of women and a shit-shooting cluster of men then was nearly plowed over when some guy carrying three pints turned without warning.

But then there was an arm around my shoulders, a chest against my back, and Kace's scent in my nose.

"Babe," he murmured in my ear.

"Kace," I murmured back.

"Missed you."

Warm fuzzies filled me as he led me through the bar and over to my stool. As in, it was officially *my* stool. A little sign that said reserved on the bar top, and a cover printed with *For Brooke* on the seat.

"Brent," he said and helped me up. "Wish I'd thought of it."

The last was a grumble that made me smile. Not here, but still stirring shit. "Thanks for the save," I murmured and reached into my backpack to unearth the foil-wrapped package of pumpkin bread. "Chocolate and pumpkin."

His eyes lit up then dimmed. "You made this?"

Oh fuck.

I bit my lip, released it. "Um . . . yeah? When I made the lasagna, I saw this recipe and remembered how good it was, and you said you liked chocolate and pumpkin so"—I shrugged—"I went to the store. I mean, you don't have to eat it. I just thought that you might like—"

Suddenly, I wasn't on the stool any longer. I was on my feet, and Kace was hauling me toward the exit.

Was he kicking me out? Maybe he'd been joking about the pumpkin/chocolate combo?

But then I had bigger problems because my bag was on the bar and unattended, and I think I already established how my whole life was inside it.

"My backpack!" I said, digging my heels in. "I can't leave it."

He froze, released me, and blue eyes filled with ice, ordered me to, "Stay."

I frowned, opening my mouth to tell him to cool it with the orders, but he was already gone, the foil-wrapped bread still in one hand. He reached my bag in a few strides, picked it up, and tucked it behind the counter, and while his movements were jerky, as though he were riding the edge of his control, he was still gentle with my precious cargo.

Then he was back, taking my hand, dragging me out of the bar and down the hallway into his office.

Or, at least, I hoped it was his office, since he kept taking me back there *and* he knew the combination to the safe. This time he didn't slam the door and pin me to it, but he did close it softly before setting the bread down on the desk like it was either the most fragile object in the world or a dangerous, ticking time bomb.

I couldn't get a read on his mood.

Quiet, but not cold like I'd thought.

Withdrawn.

With an edge of panic?

He faced me, leaning back on the desk, and closed his eyes. Then he sucked in a breath. Every instinct was telling me that he was riding the edge, that he might blow and lash out—thanks,

Steven for that, for teaching me that a man in pain would hurt me. I was trained to keep my distance, out of fear and safety, and because *I* was scared of this thing between us.

But I was also jumping in.

And I knew that Kace was different.

So, I pushed off the door and went to him, wrapping my arms around his waist and holding on tight. "What happened?"

He'd jumped at the contact, and I expected a barb. Instead, I got sweet. His chin rested on top of my head. "I mentioned that I grew up in the system," he said softly. "I didn't mention that I was in there from the time I was two. Bounced from house to house, my mom's and into foster care, a family member's and back into foster care, then the family part stopped, and it was just foster parent to foster parent. Eventually, I landed in a group home, and that was its own special kind of hell."

"Baby," I murmured.

It was a recitation on the surface, withdrawn facts, but listening to him, I realized what I'd heard in the bar, what I'd seen below the superficial words. Old pain. Aching hurts that never fully healed, no matter how hard you tried to get on with life.

Kace had that, and I realized that was part of why I was so comfortable with him. He understood what I'd gone through, and even though his pain was different than mine, the outcome was the same, and it wasn't something we would ever fully recover from. It wouldn't stop us from living our lives, but it would creep into it at odd moments, try to steal the good times and happiness.

And sometimes it would win.

Not every time.

But sometimes.

"Never," he said. "Never has someone done this, made something for me, given me something because they thought I'd like it. Not my mom or dad, not my foster parents, not the women I dated. But you"—he leaned back slightly and cupped my cheek—"three days with you and you did that, you gave that. No strings, just because I might like it."

"Baby."

He shuddered. "I knew you were good when you walked through the door. I fucking knew it. Couldn't keep my eyes off you, switched the sides of the bar I worked at so I could be close and none of the other fuckers working here could." I jerked in his hold, lips twitching at the admission. "But, babe . . . I didn't have it in me to hope that you might give me good without strings or games or fucking with my head." His eyes slipped closed again, and I felt mine get wet. "I sure as fuck never dared to dream that I could have something that pure."

That was the most incredible thing someone had ever said to me, and I didn't know how to respond, I just knew I was going to try. "Kace—"

A knock sounded at the door.

"Sorry to interrupt," came a male voice, "but I'm losing control out here."

"Fuck," he muttered. Then louder, "One minute and I'll be out."

I sighed.

He took one look at my face. "I'm sorry to dump this on you and leave, but—"

"It's your job."

"*Babe.*" Kace's palm convulsed, and I couldn't read the expression that crossed his face, not withdrawn any longer, not in the least, but it was gone so quickly I couldn't process it.

"Go."

I stepped back and opened the door. "I'll—"

I was going to say that I would meet him in there, but before I could finish my sentence, he snagged my hand and tugged me along behind him. Which gave me way too many dog-on-a-leash vibes.

"I can walk on my own, you know."

"Know it," Kace muttered. "Like to hold your hand."

Oh.

Oh.

I shut up, trailed him into the bar.

And I did it, letting him hold my hand.

SEVENTEEN

Kace

BROOKE and I were alone in the bar, the lights were dimmed, and the front door was locked.

But she was still typing.

So I'd left her to it, pressing a soft kiss to her head on the way to my office and my desk full of paperwork, trying to sneak out quietly as I'd gone.

She'd still noticed, glancing up at me with slightly hazy eyes and saying, "I'm almost done, baby."

"Take your time," I'd murmured, giving her that kiss and slipping out.

That had been an hour ago.

Now my paperwork was done, she was still typing away, and I'd broken out the pumpkin chocolate bread. Just peeling back that foil was like opening the best Christmas present of my life.

Not that I'd had many of those, but that wasn't the point.

It was the best thing I'd ever had in my mouth.

And I wasn't going to say that aloud. Ever.

"You like it?"

I glanced up, saw Brooke leaning against the doorframe, her eyes still a little hazy but a smile curving her lips.

"I think that's evident by the crumbs on my face," I murmured, wrapping the foil around the bread and pushing to my feet. "You have enough time?"

A nod. "Never, but yes."

"Walk you home?"

Her eyes softened. "Do you have any room in your stomach after eating all that bread? I have leftover lasagna and some store-bought French bread at my apartment if you want to stay for dinner . . . or whatever a meal at one in the morning might be called."

"It's almost four," I murmured. "And, yes, I'll guarantee I'll always have room for your lasagna."

"Four?"

I smiled. "Four."

"Holy—" She shook her head. "This place has good flow."

"*This* place has good inspiration for your leading men."

"I can't argue that." A beat. "So, lasagna?"

"Fuck yeah," I said and took her hand. This time she didn't protest, and we walked down the hall. I left her briefly to double-check the locks, made sure the lights were off, and then took her hand again as I set the alarm and closed the back door. After one more lock check, we were walking to her apartment.

She chatted my ear off the entire way.

The *Scream* franchise was the best scary movie franchise in history. For some strange reason, she was desperate to see the dude who was on vacation walking around in his underwear. Daises were her favorite flower, but her favorite scent was rose. And I knew this because she was a sucker for a bath and took one every day with fancy bath shit.

I made a mental note to pick up some of that fancy bath shit, along with checking the schedule of the local one-screen theater. It was nearing Halloween and they always showed classic horror flicks. If *Scream* was showing soon, I was taking Brooke.

By the time I'd decided that, we were at her apartment.

Or at least, walking up the final set of stairs that led to her door.

I was just reaching around her to unlock that door when I noticed the shadow. My reaction was pure instinct, and I grabbed Brooke's waist, shoving her behind me. The shadow rose, growing and coalescing into a person.

A man. Tall and broad and with a mean fucking look on his face.

Which was why I handed Brooke my keys and ordered, "Go into your apartment, lock the door, call the police."

She didn't move.

"*Babe.*"

The man's face got even meaner.

"Steven?"

Brooke's voice was surprised, but also soft, and that pissed me off. If this was Steven the ex, then she had absolutely no reason to have any sort of softness for the prick.

"Brooke."

Terse. Cold. Angry.

My shoulders stiffened, and I took a step toward the door, taking Brooke along with me. "Inside, babe," I said softly.

"She's not your fucking babe!"

Mean went to crazy and I had to admit, I hadn't expected this turn of events. Brooke had described what happened between her and her ex, but she hadn't mentioned him still being around or showing up at her apartment in the middle of the night. Frankly, I'd expected that Tabitha would create this kind of scene, not Brooke's ex from ten years before.

"Steven."

Brooke's voice wasn't soft now.

"You left," she accused. "When I needed you the most, you just fucking left."

"Brooke—"

"So, tell me," she snapped. "Why in the fuck are you here now?"

Steven's eyes shot to my right, to where she'd moved out from behind me. I fought the urge to yank her back mainly because the expression on her face had gone straight from shooting daggers into tossing grenades.

She was pissed.

Damn right she was pissed. This fucker had shot her when she was down, hurt her at her most vulnerable. He shouldn't be showing his face in her presence, not now, not fucking ever.

"Go the fuck home and do not ever *fucking* come back."

"Brookie," he slurred. "We were young, and I made a mistake. I shouldn't have let you go. Not when you were the best thing I'd ever had." He took a stumbling step toward her, the scent of alcohol filling the air. "But I've changed. My wife left—"

"Your wife?" Brooke gasped. "You're married and you're *here*?"

"She *left!*" he screamed.

Brooke snorted. "And how'd *that* feel?"

"It—" He shook his head, eyes dilated. "If you can just understand—"

Okay, no. She wasn't going to understand anything.

I shifted so I was between the asshole and my woman.

"It's late," she said. "I'll give you my number—"

"Not happening," I snapped.

Brooke put her hand on my arm. "Steven, it's late. We'll set up another time to talk when it's not the middle of the night."

"It wouldn't be the middle of the fucking night if you hadn't left me, hadn't made me track you down and then not come home until four-o-fucking-clock in the morning!" His voice boomed through the halls, and I went from really annoyed to really *fucking* annoyed.

What a bag of dicks.

"You had almost a decade to find me, Steven," Brooke said, voice hard. "You couldn't honestly think that one night of showing up out of the blue—"

Rage turned his features ugly. "You always were such a stuck-up bitch—"

And yeah, *that* was when I'd reached my limit.

"Look, dude," I said. "You need to leave."

He shoved his finger in my face. "You need to shut your fucking mouth and leave my woman alone."

Brooke shifted at my spine. "You're fucking kidding me, right?" she snapped. "I haven't seen you in almost ten years, and then you show up unannounced—*and* I have no idea how you even found me since my address is unlisted, by the way—"

"You think you're so fucking smart, but you're not. It's right there, your address, right on your domain." He staggered closer. "Not smart enough to realize that, you fucking bitch."

Before that moment, I'd had enough.

After him calling my woman a fucking bitch, I lost it.

And I lost it making two huge mistakes.

"Go inside, Brooke," I growled and launched myself at the asshole. He was bigger than me, but I had sobriety to go along with my fury. We hit the ground with a thud that I chased with a fist to his face. The *crack* of his nose was fucking satisfying, along with his cry of pain. He got in a shot to my ribs that hurt like hell, but then I got the advantage and landed a series of blows to his torso and face.

"Stop," Brooke shouted.

I blocked a punch. "Inside. Now."

"No," she said. "You can't—"

Steven lurched, almost knocking me off, but I had body position, and I had him pinned with my legs.

"Call the fucking police." I shoved my elbow into his throat, not lightly, and he started choking. Not my fucking problem. That this asshole would come here, basically stalk her, and then show up blitzed out of his mind and pissed off at Brooke having a life . . . it was insanity, and I was going to make sure the asshole saw it my way and never came back.

"Kace—"

I reared back, wanting to make eye contact to make sure she understood that I had this, that I was going to make Steven see reason, but I wasn't going to lose my fucking mind and kill the bastard.

Tempting, but I wouldn't give him the satisfaction.

Besides, jail didn't have lasagna and chocolate pumpkin bread.

Unfortunately, I didn't realize how close Brooke was and the moment I leaned back and spun, trying to get a lock on her gaze, I felt my shoulder make contact.

With her face.

With her nose.

First mistake.

Immediately, her nose began bleeding and she fell back with a cry, both hands over her face.

I punched Steven once more, shoved him away, and rushed over to her.

"Babe," I said. "Fuck. Are you okay?" My hands dropped gently to her shoulders, and I tried to tug her arms away. "Let me see."

"I'm fine." Her voice was muffled. "I shouldn't have gotten so close."

I managed to peel back one hand. *"Fuck."* Already bruising. I must have hit her just right. "I'm so sorry, babe. We need ice on that five minutes ago."

She nodded, started to push to her feet.

I'd already made my second mistake. I just didn't know it yet.

Not until the blinding pain across my skull penetrated, not until the darkness rose up and seized me.

EIGHTEEN

Brooke

KACE GROANED when the doorbell rang.

Two days had passed since he'd gotten the concussion to end all concussions.

Two days since my fucking crazy ex had shown up on my doorstep and knocked him over the head with a potted plant.

Two days Kace had been in my bed, but I hadn't been able to enjoy it because I'd been so worried about his injury that I was scared to touch him wrong. Also, the brace around my severely bruised, though thankfully not broken nose had made just breathing difficult, let alone planning any seduction feasible.

Black lace had failed.

The lasagna had stayed in the fridge and the police had shown. Turned out, my chainsaw neighbor friend could actually be a little useful because he'd heard the commotion and called them.

That was good.

Black lace failing was not.

Me barely being able to look at Kace because I felt beyond guilty that my ex had attacked him in the middle of the night was also not good.

Him barely being able to disguise his disgust when he looked at me wasn't great either.

But I owed it to him to at least get him healthy.

And then I'd let him go.

Remove the crazy from his life. I'd just figured the crazy would come from me, from my head and insecurities, not from some specter of the past I'd never expected to lay eyes on again.

"I got it," I said, pushing to my feet and hurrying to answer the door.

"DoorDash," he muttered, sitting up.

"What?" I stopped

"Couldn't let you cook me another meal, babe." He held up his phone. "So, delivery."

This time a knock accompanied the bell and he winced. Shit, the noise couldn't be good for his head. I moved to the door, checked the peephole, and tugged it open. Sure enough, it was delivery, and it smelled fucking incredible. I thanked the person and grabbed the bags, then used my foot to close the door.

Then I turned to Kace.

He winced.

My heart sank.

Carefully, I brought the bags to the kitchen and set them on the counter. "You know you don't have to do this, right?"

He pushed off the couch. "Do what?"

"This pity thing." I shook my head firmly. "I'm fine if you want to bail. I get it. My life fucked you up and you want to leave—"

"What the fuck are you talking about?"

I jumped.

"You—"

"You think I want to bail?"

I rolled my eyes. "You can barely look at me. Like I said, I understand. It's fine. We had a nice moment and—"

The hand pressed to my mouth, both startling me into silence and effectively muting future words. "Why in the ever-loving fuck would I want to leave?" He shook his head, no wince this time. "I told you about my childhood, told you about how little good I had. You—*you* are the one good thing I've managed to snag, and I sure as fuck am not letting you go."

I shoved him away. "But you've spent the last two days not looking at me, flinching from my touch, and when you do deign to actually make eye contact, your expression tells me that I'm torturing you."

"Babe."

"You've barely been able to stand being in the same room—"

"Babe."

"What?" I snapped.

"It's not you, it's me."

I nearly threw that bag of Chinese food at his head. *It's not you, it's me.* Was the motherfucker serious because—

Then he kept talking, and I was really glad that I didn't waste that delicious-smelling food by launching it at him.

"*I* did that to you. I left you unprotected with that fucking prick. *I'm* the reason you have two shiners and a broken nose—"

"It's not broken—"

Blue eyes locked on mine. "I hurt you."

Oh.

Oh.

I got it now.

Shit. I'd missed it before, missed the fact that my alpha male was beating himself up because he thought he'd failed to protect me. Instead, I'd defaulted right back to my same old insecurities, thinking he couldn't possibly want me, and by doing so, I'd nearly ruined it.

I stepped around the counter and got close. "I'm realizing now that I fucked up."

Kace grunted.

"Really fucked up."

"I know it'll take time for you to believe in us and to build something totally impenetrable to the self-doubt that eats you . . . but, babe, I've been gone for you since the moment I laid eyes on that gorgeous face. I'm not trying to find a way out, I'm trying to find a way in." He wrapped an arm around my waist, tugged me flush against him. "I like being in. I want to get deeper. I want to be so deep inside that you'll never be able to cut me loose."

Warm words chasing out the cold of the last two days.

But truthfully? The warm words with all those mentions of deep and deeper were getting to me in another way.

"Also, I got the landlord to repair your buzzer system," he said. "No more permanently unlocked building door means fewer surprises."

More warm.

Also, more heat with him pressing me so firmly against him. The contact was perfect, but it also wasn't platonic. My lady parts were awake and interested and didn't give one shit that my nose was still in a bandage.

I shifted slightly, hips moving against his.

"Babe."

"I was wearing black lace two nights ago," I told him. "Planned on plying you with chocolate and bread and lasagna and jumping your bones." His cock stirred, hardening against my abdomen, and I plastered myself against him. "I don't have lace on today, but maybe I don't need it?"

"*Babe.*"

I rose on tiptoe and fitted myself against him, pelvis tilting, the contact making stars flash.

"I don't think I need lace. I just need you," I murmured.

Silence.

"And your big, beautiful co—"

He swung me up into his arms, making me squeal, but immediately I tried to squirm away. "Your head, Kace. I don't want—"

"Shutting you up now."

"What—?"

He kissed me, taking advantage of the fact that my mouth was open and shoving his tongue deep inside. But inside of controlled heat and careful touches, Kace was a man possessed. He plundered my mouth as he carried me into the bedroom, and though he set me gently on the bed, he also didn't waste a second in stripping my pajama pants and T-shirt from my body.

"Kill me with these," he muttered, shrugging out of his shirt. "Every fucking time." His sweats hit the floor. "So fucking thin, I swear I can see your tits and pussy right through them."

Since they *were* old, that was probably accurate.

"Teasing me, then making me feel like a sick fuck for wanting to fuck you while you're hurting."

"I'm not hurting."

Which basically translated to me begging him to please, for the love of all the carbs in my kitchen, fuck me. And to do it well.

Based on the look in Kace's eyes, I didn't have any doubt that would happen.

He produced a condom from somewhere, rolled it on, and then kissed me until I was gasping for breath. When I broke away to suck in oxygen, his mouth trailed to my breasts, sucking a nipple deeply and making me arch off the bed. Pleasure shot down my spine, bloomed between my thighs, and I was wet, wetter than I'd ever been in my life. I needed him inside. Now.

Kace didn't seem to care because he stayed at my breasts, sucking them roughly, rolling them between his fingertips, basically reducing me to a pile of mush.

Then he kissed me some more.

The desperate, plundering kiss that made my head spin like I was the one with the concussion.

But when he began sliding down again, his mouth trailing over my abdomen, I'd had enough teasing. I loved his mouth, loved what it had done to my pussy a week before, but I didn't need a mouth, I needed his cock deep inside, and I needed it pounding hard.

I wove my fingers into his hair and yanked his head up to mine.

Probably not smart when my man had a concussion, but I wasn't thinking straight. And Kace didn't seem to mind. "Now, baby," I murmured and wrapped my legs around his hips, arching up, trying to get him where I needed him.

His sexy smile.

His incredible eyes.

And then his cock sliding inside.

"*Babe.*"

I was right there with him. He was perfect. *We* were perfect together.

Then he began to move.

And somehow it all got more perfect.

We were in sync, and he could read my body almost better than I could myself, anticipating changing angles and pressure until finally I was climbing the peak, heat swirling through my limbs, pleasure growing between my thighs, his thumb stroking my clit.

"Yes," I gasped when he knew I needed more, needed it harder before I could beg for it. "Don't stop."

"Babe."

"Please," I sobbed, hips moving against him, my head thrown back onto the pillow. "Baby. *Oh God.*"

"*Babe.*"

I was close. So fucking close that I could feel my orgasm swirling just below the surface.

He bent and nipped the corner of my mouth.

I hadn't realized I'd been biting down on it, hadn't realized that little corner could fill me with heat. Not until Kace. His teeth on that spot sent me over the edge, thighs tightening, moan long and loud, pleasure bursting out from my clit and fanning flames throughout my body.

He stroked into me two, three more times before his own orgasm had him, then we were both sailing down the other side of the precipice.

I'd known it was going to be good between us.

I'd known it was going to be the best.

I just hadn't known how good.

Which is why I burst into tears. It was too good, too perfect. I didn't know how I'd existed in a world without Kace, and I felt so lucky to have him in my life.

"*Babe.*"

I kept crying. Emotional and happy and tears leaking all over the place because that orgasm had stolen my common sense.

"I love you."

My tears dried up.

What the—

"Waited a lifetime for this, for you in my bed, and I'm not

going to be shy about letting you know." He brushed the mois-ture off my cheeks. "You're perfect, just the way you are." A beat. "Even if you're distracting me from really good Chinese and snotting against my chest."

I sat up, almost clanking our foreheads together, which would have been really bad for the concussion. "The food!"

Kace burst out laughing. "Not the snot?"

I sniffed. "You deserved it, being too sweet and too perfect."

"Babe," he murmured.

"And you have to know that I love you, too. I didn't know it until I saw Steven in that hall, until I realized how different you are from him, how different *I* am when I'm with you." I touched his cheek. "I'm not awkward, you don't care what I wear—"

"Prefer you naked," he grunted.

I smiled. "Like that," I said and pressed a soft kiss to his lips. "And I like *you*. Thanks for taking me as I am."

"Babe."

"Now, Chinese." I started to squirm out from under him.

"*Babe.*"

I stopped. "What?"

Okay, it was a little churlish, but I'd orgasmed, I'd cried, I'd shared, now I needed some fried rice.

"Stay here and I'll get the food." He pushed out of the bed, slipping into the bathroom for a few seconds to take care of the condom—and then a few more to wash his hands—thank you relationship gods for the perfect man. "Scary movie on TV," he ordered when he came back through.

My eyes stung again.

"No more crying!" he called.

I sighed.

I smiled.

Kace was perfect. Perfect for me.

"Crying is a perfectly acceptable emotional response to the

man I've always dreamed of suddenly making an appearance in my life."

A beat of quiet, then, "I'll bring tissues, too."

And because I was perfect for Kace right back, I said, "I've already got a box on my nightstand.

"*Babe.*"

EPILOGUE

Kace, Christmas Eve

BOBBY'S WAS CROWDED, my woman was on her stool, typing away, and Brent was handling his end of the bar without giving me too much shit. Patrons were gathered around the bar, clustered around tables, chowing down on wings and guzzling beers, and doing it all with smiles on their faces.

Best night ever.

That was mostly because Brooke was there, glancing up from her laptop occasionally and smiling at me.

But it was also because of the email in my inbox.

Heather had delivered.

Bobby's was fifty percent mine.

Profits were up, slow times were no longer slow, and—

I had so much more than I ever could have dreamed of. A job I enjoyed, an apartment that shared a wall with a chainsaw-snoring neighbor that I tolerated because it meant that I could go to bed every night with my woman, *and* it was close to the bar. But most of all, I had Brooke.

Twelve months now.

Twelve months since I'd felt that jolt.

Six since I'd finally given in.

Six wasted . . . and yet, not. Because Brooke and I were together, we were happy, and we'd seen the Underwear Guy, whose real name was actually Frank, and he was hilarious, although he was a street performer and not actually on vacation. Still, neither of us could tell if he was serious about that or if it was just another fib to throw us off. Which Brooke absolutely loved, because it gave her a bunch of outrageous material for her novels. Lie or not, I was just thrilled that I finally had good.

A good woman.

A good job.

A good life.

I'd known shit and so I appreciated the good.

But I still wasn't buying Brooke a pet pig, even if it had become her life's dream since seeing one on a vet show she was obsessed with. Seeming to read the train of my thoughts, Brooke glanced up at me, her expression immediately pleading.

"Babe."

She stuck out her bottom lip. "They're super smart."

"*Babe.*"

She pouted.

"I love you," I murmured and refilled her glass with Diet Coke she wouldn't drink.

"I know."

"Still no pig." A kiss to the top of her head. "Now get to work and hit that deadline. We have important Christmas plans to get to tomorrow."

"Like what? Watching action movies and gorging on popcorn because it's your turn to pick what we put on?"

"Yes." I grinned. "Exactly. Plus sex. Lots and lots of sex."

She wrinkled her nose. "Your *sex* is the reason I'm behind on this deadline."

"You love me."

Brooke sighed. "I do."

"And my cock."

"Kace!" Her cheeks flared hot and she reached across the bar to smack me, but I stole her hand and pressed a kiss to her palm.

"Love you, babe."

She smiled. "Love you, too, gorgeous." Then she winked. "All parts of you."

I burst out laughing and as I made my way down the bar, filling drinks, pulling bills, adding to tabs, I knew exactly how lucky I was.

I had good.

And I was never letting it go.

VIRGIN DAIQUIRI

Brent

I SMILED at Brooke and Kace, or rather, Brooke settled into her computer while Kace stared at her like she owned his heart.

Because she did.

Still, it was Christmas Eve, last call was done, the bar was empty and clean. Which meant my duties were done. It was time for me to go back to my apartment and go to sleep.

Pathetic?

Maybe.

But I'd gotten used to being alone.

Better that way.

I waved to Kace and slipped quietly by Brooke, not wanting to disrupt her flow. Technically, I'd known her longer and I still felt real guilt at not having kept in touch with her after Hayden died. I should have looked after her better.

But the past was the past and I, more than anyone, understood that it belonged there.

Sighing, I stretched my aching back—reason one I'd gotten out of the military—and walked away from the bar. I'd just reached the doorway to the hall when a tiny female crashed into him.

"Oof," I grunted, instinctively reaching out to steady her. "Easy there, darlin'."

She stiffened and pulled back. "I'm sorry," she said, and my gut clenched from the impact. Her voice was sweet summer peaches, warm honey dripping down fingers. It was the most intoxicating thing I'd ever heard. "I should have been more careful."

"You're fine, darlin'."

She nodded, lifting her hand to push her bangs from her face. It was trembling, as was her voice when she went on. "I left my purse. I can't believe I was so stupid to—"

"What color was it?" I asked gently.

"Black with a gold zipper and chain."

I nodded. "I have it. Come on," I said. "I saw it left behind earlier and put it in the office." I'd seen it on Kace's desk earlier while on break.

Her relief was palpable. "Thank you so much. I swear, my whole life is in that bag."

"Your whole life?"

She smiled and it was another punch to the stomach. I had the distinct thought that I wanted to see that smile forever. *What?* Blinking away the insane idea, I turned and led her down the hall, opening the door marked private and pointing to the desk.

Her hands came up and she clasped them to her chest.

"Oh, thank God."

"You come here often, darlin'?" I asked and mentally winced at the words, which came out sounding like a lame pickup line.

"No," she said. "I just moved to town."

"Ah. You going to come back in tomorrow?"

Her cheeks went a little pink. "Um. You guys are open on Christmas Day?"

Oh. Shit. Now I'd gone from lame to sounding like a total idiot. "Oh. Um. No, we're not. I . . . forgot."

"You forgot Christmas?" she asked, stepping forward to pick up her purse.

I shrugged. "No family here. Not a ton to celebrate."

"Oh."

And now I could add pathetic to the list.

But then she glanced up and him and I saw warmth in her gorgeous brown eyes. "You could come over to my house. I was going to cook and—"

The warmth in her eyes died.

Probably because my face was coming across as shocked. Or maybe a little disbelieving. Who invited a strange man back to their house? Moreover, who invited a strange *black* man to their house?

That had happened to me exactly . . . never.

"Never mind," she said. "It was a stupid idea."

I huffed out a laugh.

"I'm *not* stupid."

"Inviting strange men you don't know isn't exactly smart."

"You're not a strange man," she said. "You're the man who saved my life by keeping my purse safe." Her chin came up and that small show of spine was the third punch to my gut. "Serial killers don't rescue purses."

I snorted. "Whatever you say, darlin'."

"I'm new in town and don't have any family and you seem nice, so I invited you for dinner." She tossed up her hands. "What exactly is the problem with that?"

"Because sweet little girls like you don't invite men like *me* places."

Her brows drew together. "Men like you?"

I rolled my eyes. "Men"—I pointed at my face—"like me."

She disappeared. I literally had no other word to describe it, but one second, she was all fire and the next, she was a blank slate. "Girls like me," she repeated, and her voice was no longer sweet peaches and sticky honey. It was ice. "I see. Heaven forbid a *girl like me* ask out a handsome man because a *girl like me* should be at home knitting or collecting cats or darning my socks." She sighed and turned away. "Or at the very least, hanging her star on a man who fits her. Someone plain and dumpy and average-looking."

Um. What?

"You're far from average-looking, darlin'."

She winced like I'd punched her.

But I wasn't blowing smoke. This woman was small and curvy with delicate features. Her eyes were a deep brown I'd never seen before and her blond hair was lush and thick, hanging in silky waves down her back. Too much sweet in a small package.

And too much sweet for him.

"Reading you loud and clear," she muttered. "Don't need to hit below the belt. I'm going back to my empty house and back to my imaginary cats."

Fuck. Someone needed to save this woman from herself.

That someone couldn't be me.

But that still didn't stop me from snagging her arm and rotating her to face me. "You live near the city now. You have to be smart." Her lips parted again, probably to tell me she *was* smart, but I kept talking. "*Street* smart. You can't tell strange men you live alone *or* invite them back to your place."

"Fine," she said.

"Fine," I agreed.

But I didn't let her go.

Her eyes flicked over my shoulder, to the ceiling, and my

gaze followed hers, half-expecting to see a giant spider dangling there.

Instead, I saw mistletoe.

I glanced back down. She licked her lips.

And suddenly, I knew she was thinking the same thing as me. Warm bodies pressed together, lips only inches apart, heat filling the space, and a kiss-inducing plant overhead.

"Mistletoe," she whispered and licked her lips again.

Just one taste.

I could give myself that.

I bent my head and slanted my mouth across hers.

VIRGIN DAIQUIRI

COMING JUNE 29TH, 2020

Get your copy of Virgin Daiquiri at
https://www.elisefaber.com/virgin-daiquiri

Want a free bonus story? Hate missing Elise's new releases?
Love contests, exclusive excerpts and giveaways?
Then signup for Elise's newsletter here!
https://www.elisefaber.com/newsletter

And join Elise's fan group, the Fabinators https://www.
facebook.com/groups/fabinators for insider information, sneak
peaks at new releases, and fun freebies! Hope to see you there!

Love After Midnight (**all stand alone**)

Rum And Notes

Virgin Daiquiri

On The Rocks

Sex On The Seats

ALSO BY ELISE FABER

Billionaire's Club (all stand alone)

Bad Night Stand

Bad Breakup

Bad Husband

Bad Hookup

Bad Divorce

Bad Fiancé

Bad Boyfriend

Bad Blind Date

Bad Wedding

Bad Engagement

Bad Bridesmaid

Bad Swipe

Bad Girlfriend

Bad Best Friend

Bad Billionaire's Quickies

Gold Hockey (all stand alone)

Blocked

Backhand

Boarding

Benched

Breakaway

Breakout

Checked

Coasting

Centered

Charging

Caged

Crashed

A Gold Christmas

Cycled

Caught

Breakers Hockey (all stand alone)

Broken

Boldly

Breathless

Ballsy (April 26,2022)

Love, Action, Camera (all stand alone)

Dotted Line

Action Shot

Close-Up

End Scene

Meet Cute

Love After Midnight (all stand alone)

Rum And Notes

Virgin Daiquiri

On The Rocks

Sex On The Seats

Life Sucks Series (**all stand alone**)

Train Wreck

Hot Mess

Dumpster Fire

Clusterf*@k

FUBAR (March 29,2022)

Roosevelt Ranch Series (**all stand alone, series complete**)

Disaster at Roosevelt Ranch

Heartbreak at Roosevelt Ranch

Collision at Roosevelt Ranch

Regret at Roosevelt Ranch

Desire at Roosevelt Ranch

Phoenix Series (**read in order**)

Phoenix Rising

Dark Phoenix

Phoenix Freed

Phoenix: LexTal Chronicles (**rereleasing soon, stand alone, Phoenix world**)

From Ashes

In Flames

To Smoke

KTS Series

Riding The Edge

Crossing The Line

Leveling The Field

Scorching The Earth

Cocky Heroes World

Tattooed Troublemaker

ABOUT THE AUTHOR

USA Today bestselling author, Elise Faber, loves chocolate, Star Wars, Harry Potter, and hockey (the order depending on the day and how well her team -- the Sharks! -- are playing). She and her husband also play as much hockey as they can squeeze into their schedules, so much so that their typical date night is spent on the ice. Elise changes her hair color more often than some people change their socks, loves sparkly things, and is the mom to two exuberant boys. She lives in Northern California. Connect with her in her Facebook group, the Fabinators or find more information about her books at www.elisefaber.com.

facebook.com/elisefaberauthor

amazon.com/author/elisefaber

bookbub.com/profile/elise-faber

instagram.com/elisefaber

goodreads.com/elisefaber

pinterest.com/elisefaberwrite

www.ingramcontent.com/pod-product-compliance
Lightning Source LLC
Chambersburg PA
CBHW052011240626
47153CB00008B/2830